EMPEROR OF ...

Book #1 In The Famous Mars Quartet

by

John Russell Fearn

1995
Gryphon Books
Brooklyn, New York
U.S.A.

EMPEROR OF MARS
by
John Russell Fearn

Acknowledgements:

EMPEROR OF MARS by John Russell Fearn, Book #1 in his famous Mars Quartet is copyright © 1950 by John Russell Fearn. Originally published in a scarce paperback edition in England in 1950. Copyright renewed by Philip Harbottle and Copyright © 1995 by Philip Harbottle. All Copyright in the literary works of John Russell Fearn is vested in Cosmos Literary Agency. For information address: 32 Tynedale Avenue, Wallsend, Tyne & Wear, England. All Rights Reserved.

Cover art specially created for this series by Ron Turner. Cover art Copyright © 1995 by Ron Turner

Introduction: "Clay Drew of Mars" by Philip Harbottle. Copyright © 1995 by Philip Harbottle.

Printing History:
First American Edition
Gryphon Books: July 1995

A Gryphon Books First Edition.

ISBN: 0-936071-47-8 $15.00

Introduction:

Clay Drew of Mars

For more than seven decades, successive generations of American readers--and indeed readers all over the world--have thrilled to the adventure novels of Edgar Rice Burroughs. In the cold light of science and astronomical discoveries, we now know that there are no wild *banths* and beautiful princesses on Mars. No teeming jungles on Venus. But Edgar Rice Burroughs remains in print, touching the hearts and minds of each new generation of fantasy fans. The answer to this contradiction is that what <u>was</u> once read as science fiction can now be enjoyed as <u>fantasy</u>...always provided that the original author had imagination and talent.

Back in 1949, the British publisher W.H. Allen struck gold when he began reissuing Edgar Rice Burroughs novels in paperback. Their appearance paved the way for the British science fiction boom which took off in 1950, fuelled by the launch of the "Vargo Statten" paperback science fiction novels written by John Russell Fearn. Fearn was an English author who had learned his craft in the American pulp magazines, many of his stories appearing alongside the works of Edgar Rice Burroughs in the pages of **Amazing Stories** and **Fantastic Adventures**.

These two strands came together in the Fall of 1950, when UK. publishers Hamilton & Co. (Stafford) Ltd. hit upon the idea of commissioning Fearn to write a series of books inspired by the success of ERB's John Carter of Mars sf novels. Fearn's brief was to create an up-to-date modern series: **EMPEROR OF MARS, WARRIOR OF MARS, RED MEN OF MARS,** and **GODDESS OF MARS.** Other Burroughsian elements included both green Martians, and a 'superior' race of red Martians, underground cities, lost races, monstrous life forms, a beautiful princess, and plot intrigues involving brain and body transplants. But the Fearn novels were not merely pastiches of ERB: Fearn brought to them his <u>own</u> canon of classic science fiction themes and plots which he himself had pioneered in the American pulp magazines.

The result of this combination of influences was a dynamic series that became a best-seller in the U.K. But the series was cut short when Hamilton's main publishing rival, Scion Ltd., offered Fearn a 5 year contract to write for them exclusively as Vargo Statten. Thus the Clay Drew of Mars series came to a premature end after four novels, and was never reprinted. Now rare, these books have become legendary collectors' items.

It is against this background that Gryphon Publications and myself are making them available to a new generation of ERB and fantasy adventure fans, with the added bonus of specially commissioned new artwork by Ron Turner. Turner was the original cover artist for most of the dozens of Fearn 'Vargo Statten' novels in the 1950s, and has long been recognized as the greatest sf paperback artist of that exciting period. For more details of these works and other contemporary British science fiction, interested readers are referred to my two books (with Stephen Holland) **VULTURES OF THE VOID** and **BRITISH SF PAPERBACKS AND MAGAZINES**, currently in print from Borgo Press in the U.S.A. and also available from Gryphon Publications. Just as J. Allen St. John captured the magic of ERB, so Ron Turner brilliantly portrays the sense of wonder and sf vision underlying Fearn's stories.

Fearn, like Edgar Rice Burroughs, was a born storyteller, with talent and imagination. Like John Carter, Clay Drew's adventures can now be enjoyed as fantasy adventure. This new Gryphon Books series is sure to become a collector's item, and is one no ERB and fantasy fan will want to miss!

Philip Harbottle, Wallsend, England, Jan. 1995

CHAPTER ONE.

THE FLYING SAUCERS.

Clayton Drew was quite convinced of one thing: he had to climb Helvellyn, the frowning Lake District Mountain beloved of all daredevils. Not that Clayton Drew was a mountaineer, or that he had any real inclination to become one. It was just that he had got to do it.

The urge came upon him in June, 1952, and from that moment he made everything bend towards his vacation in August. He booked his room at a Lakeland hotel, spent several weeks buying climber's tackle, and had nothing to do then but pray for decent weather. His wish was granted. On August 6th he began to ascend Helvellyn, two amateur mountaineers from the hotel his only companions.

They were puzzled, and frankly admitted it. From the conversations they had had with Clayton Drew they knew he had never climbed a mountain before; but they also knew that nothing on earth would satisfy him except to reach the highest point on the peak.

Drew himself did not understand his urge, either. He tramped along through the sunny, rocky foothills, rope and tackle about him, spiked shoes digging into the hard ground, hardly speaking to the two young men who had volunteered to help him in his effort—chiefly because they were afraid he might break his neck if he tried alone.

Yes, there was something queer about it all. In the ordinary way of life Clayton Drew was an engineer, with science for his hobby. His powerful frame and craggy features were hardly in keeping with his studious pursuits. He looked more like a trained athlete than a man who spent half his life sitting down. Some of his intimates thought him a bore; girls were nothing more than acquaintances. He seemed to spend his life examining scientific or engineering mysteries with never a thought outside them. Without parents, with few friends, he was a good example of a lone wolf.

"Do you suppose," he asked, when he and his two companions had stopped to study the rearing, friendless heights of the mountain, "we can make the ascent in one day?"

His two colleagues looked at one another in wonder, then back to Drew's powerful profile, his keen blue eyes weighing up the sheer precipices and savage rocks.

"Depends," one of them said. "You're not a professional climber, Clay, so it will take you longer than it will us. We can try, of course—but what's the hurry? We've all the tackle for pitching a camp."

"I didn't come here to camp," Drew answered briefly. "I want to get to the top of Helvellyn. Come on—let's get started."

Quite convinced that he was mildly crazy his two comrades began to unwind their safety rope. All preparations were made and the ascent began—a slow, toe-and-finger-hold climb up sheer rock faces, clawing upwards into the blue of the sky, the hot sun shafting down through the eternally drifting cloudbanks.

The ascent had begun at ten in the morning. By noon some seven hundred feet had been ascended and a broad ledge gained. Here the trio paused and refreshed themselves, contemplating the patchwork far below where fields and lanes and streams lay inter-twined, the small dots of cottages and farmhouses relieving the monotony here and there.

"Look, Clay," one of the men said, setting down the

thermos flask, "there must be some reason for this climb you're trying to make. A chap doesn't suddenly decide on a job like this unless he's either a keen mountaineer or plain crazy. What's the angle ?"

Clay shook his head slowly. His rugged features were pre-occupied. Then he shrugged and pushed his hand through his untidy dark hair.

"I've got what the Yanks call a 'yen'," he responded. "I just can't help myself. Sudden phobia maybe. I developed it in June and since then I've hardly been able to think of anything except climbing this blasted mountain."

"From the way you refer to it," the other man said, "you obviously don't really want to climb it."

"I detest it," Clay admitted frankly. "I just have to, that's all."

"For a bet, maybe ?"

"No—nothing like that. Just an urge—pure and simple."

Silence—at least for a time. Silence, that is, save for the soft moaning of the wind through countless niches and crevices. Then, presently, as the three got to their feet to continue the ascent, the sound changed. It took on a deep humming as though a giant bee were loose somewhere. It became louder with the seconds, having something of the persistency of a humming-top.

"What the devil's that ?" one of the men demanded finally, looking about him and then at the drifting citadels of cumulus cloud. "It sounds like a queer type of 'plane, or else a . . . . . Great heavens, look !" he broke off, pointing.

His instruction was unnecessary. His companion and Clay were both gazing fixedly at an object sweeping down from the heights. Now and again the clouds hid it, but at each revelation it was much lower in altitude, and as it came nearer the deafening drone increased. It was like an enormous cartwheel, spokes radiating from perimeter to hub. It glittered in the sunlight with the sheen of gold.

"It's a flying saucer !" Clay ejaculated suddenly, staring

in amazement; then he whipped out field-glasses from the case on his shoulder and focussed them quickly.

Under the power of the lenses the speeding object took on pin sharp detail. He could see now that the "spokes" of the thing were actually as transparent as glass and there seemed to be tiny objects moving in the midst of them like living flies in amber. The "hub" had deeply sunken portholes; whilst the outer rim, also transparent, contained what seemed to be machinery.

So much the three astounded men had time to notice, then the object hurtled past them overhead, pursuing an unerring straight line through the narrow pass and sweeping upwards with feather-light ease upon reaching the end of it.

"Flying saucer is right!" declared the climber next to Clay. "I thought those things vanished two years ago. Quite a flock of them at one time—supposed to be, anyway —but nobody ever got near enough to examine them."

"Those other ones had exhaust trails, though," the other man said. "I remember reading about them . . . ."

"It's coming back," Clay interrupted. "And lower down, too. If we don't watch ourselves we're liable to get hurt."

Spinning round on itself in the most extraordinary fashion the flying saucer dropped some fifty feet in twenty-five seconds, then came whizzing back with a scream of hidden power engines. The blast of air it split as it came past sent all three men reeling back against the wall of the ledge. Hardly had they straightened than the saucer began to return yet again—lower still.

"It's an attack!" one of the men said desperately. "If we don't get into rock protection we'll . . . . ."

He got no further. The saucer flashed by, no more than thirty feet overhead. At the same instant, something the colour of lavender jetted from the outer rim of the thing. It seemed to be some kind of beam. Whatever its nature the hapless climber stood no chance. He was blasted clean out of existence and the ledge was as bare as though he had never been there.

Clay exchanged a dazed look with the remaining man. Both of them were too horrified to think straight—then, so rapidly that Clay hardly had time to realise it, the lavender beam struck again as the saucer came hurtling back. Clay saw smoke and flame explode round the man a foot or two from him, and he himself was flung to the ground by a savage electric shock. Half paralysed, conscious of the fact that the second man had been utterly disintegrated, he lay staring at the golden wheel as it twisted and twirled like a flung discus on its journey back to him.

He closed his eyes, expecting death—but it did not come. Instead something invisible gripped him and he was whirled from the ledge into space. He fully anticipated plunging on the rocks below, but instead he remained in mid air, perhaps ten feet under the rim of the weird flyer. He could not move a single muscle. He was compelled to submit as, very slowly, he began to rise upwards towards the flyer, during the course of which it hurtled out of the pass and travelled ever higher over the mountain peaks.

Half conscious, battered by the wind, sickened with his ghastly floating in space, Clay became aware of hands seizing him. He was dragged into what appeared gloomy darkness after the sunlight reflecting from clouds. Then everything seemed deathly quiet, except for the remote throbbing of immensely powerful engines.

Slowly he got to his feet, his eyes accustoming to gloom. He discovered that light was coming from a single yellow globe set high in a metallic ceiling. Apparently he was within some kind of small chamber with a trap in the floor, through which he had been dragged. His captors, as well as he could discern them, were tall well-built men in dark one piece costumes which covered them from throat to feet.

"What goes on ?" he demanded in sudden anger. "You killed my two friends out there, and now you've kidnapped me ? Who's running this damned saucer, anyway ?"

"If you will please step this way," one of the men murmured, and he seemed extraordinarily deferential.

Clay hesitated, then realised he had no choice. A door in the metal wall had been opened. He stepped into a narrow corridor and found it was transparent on all sides. Dizziness assailed him for a moment as infinitely far beneath his feet he saw the landscape spread out. But it was not just the Lake District: It was all England in a relief map. Then there was the Atlantic, and the hazy outline of America. He was many miles up in the air.

"Keep walking," advised the man immediately behind him. "If you sense vertigo look straight ahead of you. We are accustomed to these transparent, radiation-proof corridors."

Clay glanced behind him. The man was immediately in the rear, his three colleagues visible beyond. All of them were unusually good looking with sharply cut features, blue eyes, and firmly brushed, black hair. They were so identical they looked like quadruplets. About them was an unmistakable air of dignity; certainly not the tough attitude of men who had organised an abduction.

"You are wondering what this is all about, of course," the man at Clay's shoulder said. "Please continue moving and matters will be explained."

So Clay advanced again, keeping his gaze straight ahead upon a gleaming metal door. As he walked he was aware of two things. One was that the machine in which he moved was rising all the time, and at a prodigous speed; and the other was that he was in one of the "spokes" of the vast wheel. The door in the distance was presumably fixed in the "hub."

When it was reached his guardian opened it quickly and then stood aside. Clay walked into an enormous room, magnificently furnished—though everything was of metal—and lighted by some concealed system which threw no shadows and which appealed to his engineering talents.

His guardians retired, closing the door gently, and he was left to survey. The carpet was thick under his feet and made of some type of fibre which defied analysis. The walls seemed to be gold-painted, or else were treated with a chemical which was glittering yellow. There were chairs, divans, enormous hassocks, rugs—and also a gigantic desk containing all manner of instruments.

Clay advanced again, absorbing the wealth and scientific power the room suggested. He gained the desk and stood contemplating small but complicated instrument panels which were unlike anything he had ever seen before. He was too interested to be frightened, and in any case the quiet dignity of his captors had satisfied him that perhaps they would at least spare his life even if they had ruthlessly picked off his colleagues on the mountain face.

As nothing seemed to happen he finally wandered to the window, deeply sunken in cast metal framework, and peered outside. The view gave him the shock of his life. Below was a gigantic green ball with a bulging equator and somewhat flattened poles in which all landscape had merged into common colour, except for a thin crescent of indigo where the night rode the Earth.

Astonished, Clay looked upwards and outwards. The blue of the sky had given place to black. Being something of a scientist he understood that the atmosphere had gone and instead the pure vacuum of interstellar void had been reached . . . . . The blackness was beyond description, more absolute that platinum dust itself, upon which were sprinkled endless myraids of coldly glittering stars, their fires no longer tremoring with the intervention of air.

The sun, blindingly incandescent, flung his ghostly corona millions of miles into emptiness; his prominences writhed with endless energy. Blinking, sun-dazzled, Clay turned his eyes away from his brief glance at the orb of day and noted the brilliantly white half moon and, inconceivably far away in space, the motionless points of the planets. Mars, Venus, Mercury—and further still the giant outer worlds. His eyes moved to the swirling, hazy infinity of light which was the Milky Way Galaxy from which Earth herself had been born—and then a soft, pleasing voice spoke close to his ear.

"You find the view interesting, Excellency ?"

Clay twirled abruptly and looked straight into the blue eyes of a man beside him. It was a highly intelligent face, elderly, with wisdom in the depthless gaze. The mouth was powerful, the nose as hooked as an eagle's. The black hair was thickly grey at the temples.

"Yes . . . very interesting." Clay spoke jerkily, noting as he did so that the man had strange insignia on his plum-coloured, one-piece tunic.

"I am Kladnor," the man explained, in his gentle way, and inclined his head slightly. "First Advisor to Her Excellency the Princess Thalia."

"Look," Clay said deliberately, " I think it's about time you explained what all this monkey business is about ! I've been so absorbed by everything I'd forgotten for the moment that you kidnapped me . . . and killed my two companions ! What is it all about . . . ." Clay paused and frowned. "Did I hear you call me 'Excellency' a moment or two ago ?"

"That is correct—Excellency."

"Then you're fawning over the wrong man," Clay said. "I've no claim to a title. I'm plain Clayton Drew, engineer, thirty years of age, and a native of London."

Kladnor smiled a little. "We know exactly who you are, my young friend, otherwise we would not have gone to such trouble to locate you. Believe me, your title is well merited. You are Emperor-Designate to the planet you call Mars."

Clay opened his mouth to speak and then shut it again. He blinked momentarily and then glanced out of the window once more.

"You . . . you mean that is where we're going ? Mars ?"

"Exactly, back to the planet whence we—my colleagues and I, that is—came. There have been others before us. For years we have been searching—for you. I believe your fellows on Earth called our visitations 'flying saucers.' It was a term we found difficult to understand."

"Are you trying to tell me that the flying saucers which

have been buzzing around for so many years have been looking for me ?" Clay demanded blankly.

"That is correct. Finally we found you . . . But come,
Excellency, please sit down. I will have a meal brought. I
am sure you must be tired."

Kladnor turned and moved silently over the rich carpet.
Clay, gazing after him, noticed that he was very tall—easily
six feet three—with stooped shoulders. It was possibly age
more than physical weakness. When he reached the desk
he moved a switch on the instrument panel, spoke a few
words in a foreign tongue, then eyed Cley steadily as he
walked over to him.

"I don't understand your language," Clay remarked,
seating himself as Kladnor motioned to a chair. "I have a
knowledge of most languages, but that's a new one."

"No, my friend, an old one," Kladnor, corrected, also
sitting down. He laced heavily jewelled hands over his
middle and added, "It is your native tongue, though you
will not be aware of it."

Cley set his jaw suddenly. "Look, Kladnor, or whatever your confounded name is, I'm getting tired of this
business ! The only thing I can remember is that you've
kidnapped me and killed two innocent men. Give me the
facts, can't you ?"

"I can—but without leading up to them they will hardly
sound credible. You, my friend, are the last surviving royal
male of Atlantis, which once existed on the continent of Mu."

"And vanished at the time of the Deluge," Clay added.
"Yes, I've read all about Atlantis. But I had nothing to
do with it. I'm an Englishman and . . . ."

"Quite so, but it is your ancestry which interests us.
Can you trace it back through thousands of years to the time
of the Deluge ?"

Clay sat back and smiled incredulously.

"Of course you cannot," Kladno continued. "But we
know all about you because an aura cannot lie. We all have
an aura, you see, and every one is different—an electrical

emanation. It is as infallible as fingerprints and is never duplicated. That is why we know you are a direct descendant, through many generations, of Hertis, one-time Emperor of Atlantis."

Kladnor paused for a moment as one of the uniformed men entered, pushing before him a rubber-wheeled affair rather like a tea trolley. He set out a meal on a nearby table and then retired. Kladnor rose, motioned, and Clay followed him to the refreshment. His mind still in a daze he found himself surveying perfectly cooked food, entirely earthly in its appearance, with a yellowish wine in a cut glass decanter.

"Please refresh yourself, Excellency," Kladnor invited. "You are not a captive, you know, but an honoured guest."

Clay took the wine handed to him, his blue eyes hard.

"All the gloss you put on it, Kladnor, doesn't alter the fact that you killed two men."

"We had nothing against those two men," the Advisor replied. "It was simply a case of being unable to get at you with our magnetic retractor without getting them too . . . . so they had to be eliminated. Ruthless, I confess, but very necessary. I would add they are the only two Earth people we have ever slain, and I trust they will be the last."

Clay began eating, then after a moment he glanced about him.

"According to my scientific belief," he said, "gravity in this ship ought to be almost non-existent, and yet we sit here as comfortably as aboard an air liner."

"It is accounted for by our velocity, Excellency. We move at a speed consistent with producing an inertia—a gravitational drag—identical with that of Earth. In space, of course, one retains a constant velocity once having achieved it because there is no resistance."

Clay ate for a while and then turned to look at the window. Dimly, far away amidst the glittering points of space, he could see the pinpoint of red which denoted Mars.

"And you mean to say I'm Emperor of that ?" he asked.

"Not yet. You will be after marrying the Princess Thalia."

Clay gave a start. "Now wait a minute ! If you think you can kidnap me and marry me off to some hag who . . ."

"A moment, Excellency." There was quiet authority in the way Kladnor raised his jewelled hand. "Let me disillusion you on one score. The Princess Thalia is a very lovely woman, and still young, but she is in the unhappy position that she cannot perpetuate the dignitaries of the Atlantean race without a husband."

"So you had to pick on me ? What's wrong with some of those upstanding lads who snatched me from Helvellyn ?"

"Only one thing : they are not of royal descent. For a dignitary to marry a commoner whilst one of royal descent still lives, even though he exist on another world, is not to be thought of. If you do not marry the Princess Thalia she will have no issue and the dignitaries of the race will die when she dies. With that the race dies too because the only rulers are those of royal birth. Without rulers any race soon descends to anarchy, revolution, destruction."

Kladnor meditated through an interval, his blue eyes fixed on distance. Clay shifted uncomfortably.

" I suppose I can ask one or two questions ?" he enquired.

"Please do. I will be glad to answer them."

"Then tell me what the people of Atlantis are doing on Mars, and why you are so sure that I am a descendant of the dignitaries."

"At the time of the Deluge," Kladnor replied, "Atlantis, and the whole continent of Mu, was overwhelmed. The Atlanteans were ruled then by Hertis. They were highly civilised and very scientific. They knew the Deluge was coming and escaped in space projectiles, settling on Mars. They domiciled themselves just below the surface of Mars so as not to interfere with the rightful inhabitants who live on the surface of their planet—and also because Hertis was prescient enough to realise that a day would come—as indeed it now has—when the surface of Mars would become too atmospherically thin to support our type of life in comfort.

"After that, life prospered for many generations, the surface Martians being too unintelligent to cause real trouble even though they hated, and still hate, our incursion into their planet. Hertis died and his son took over. So it went on until some time ago the last surviving male dignitary passed away and Princess Thalia became ruler. We realised then that she had no royal male with whom to mate. An aura test of every male revealed him to be below the required number of 6,000, which is the lowest aura to which any royal Atlantean descends."

"I don't grasp that a bit," Clay confessed, taking some wine.

"The more refined a human being, the higher the aura rate emanated," Kladnor explained. "I repeat, we could not find any male for the Princess. We were faced with disaster. If no issue followed her, trouble, as I have said, would ensue. Then, in the records, it was discovered that not all the dignitaries of Atlantis had escaped at the time of the Deluge—that is, not all of them had made the journey into space. Some might have survived the Deluge, in which case a descendent in the modern day might exist. I was ordered by the Princess to search the planet Earth for such a possibility. That brought the advent of the 'flying saucer' when we began our task."

Kladnor considered for a moment, then continued.

"Super-sensitive aura detectors in our space machines made it possible to take group readings of human beings, thousands at a time, without them being aware of it. We had nearly given up our search as hopeless when we found an aura registering 6,006. We had found a royal descendant ! The rest was easy. Two of our emissaries were landed on Earth and became, to all intents and purposes, ordinary Earth men. It was not difficult since being originally born of this planet, we have the same physique. You were traced, but in London it would have been hard to kidnap you without killing many people, who would be bound to attack us, thinking hostility was aimed at.

"So hypnotic equipment was used and a thought was planted in your brain. You must go to a lonely spot and there be abducted. You obeyed—and the rest you know."

Clay snapped his fingers. "So that's why I wanted to climb Helvellyn ! That mountain."

"Exactly. The rest is simple. You will be transported to Mars, there to wed Her Highness and fulfil your rightful destiny as a dignitary."

"Suppose I don't like the idea ? I've lived all my life on Earth, and I rather like the old planet."

"We who have duty to perform must forego our personal desires," Kladnor replied, shrugging.

"You know English pretty well," Clay commented. "And so do your colleagues."

"Is that so remarkable ? We have heard it spoken over the radio and learned it."

"Can the Princess speak it ?"

"Fluently. Remember our search has been going on for years. We took back sound-track records of our investigation, and many English speeches were included in them. You will find Her Highness most proficient."

Clay pondered for a moment, then : "You refer to me as an Emperor-designate, then to Thalia as a Princess. Isn't that wrong somewhere ?"

"Upon her marriage to you she will become Empress. You have a title above hers because you are the male—and you will also be the ruler upon marriage. She will be able to suggest, but not to command, as she does at present."

"And how is she going to like that ?"

"Because she is royal she will accept it—just as you, being royal, will accept the extraordinary situation in which you find yourself."

"Don't to be too sure of that, Kladnor."

Clay got to his feet impatiently, his meal finished. With his hands plunged into the pockets of his corduroy climbing trousers he wandered to the window again and stared into space. Earth was far away now, but Mars did not seem any bigger as yet. Then Clay turned suddenly.

"Do you realise what you're asking?" he cried. "I'm being carried across forty-million miles of space to marry a woman I've never seen and to give orders to a race I know nothing about. It's fantastic!"

"Not altogether." Kladnor got up too and walked silently across to him. There was a serious light in his blue eyes. "We need you, young man," he continued. "The Princess, for all her power, will not be able to stand alone against the Martians if they really decide one day to attack —and I think they will. They are a cruel, barbaric race and have never ceased to hate. I am uneasy at this very moment, with all the intelligentsia of Mars being away. The Princess has but a handful of inhabitants to guard her."

Clay frowned. "How many are there of you all told?"

"Three thousand. The unfit have been weeded out— and only the best remain. Those with the finest brains have become the Governing Clique, of course, under Her Highness' orders. But they do not number more than a score and they have all been busy on the search for you."

"Then this isn't the only flying saucer?"

"No." Kladnor looked out of the window. "From this position you cannot see the seven other machines following us. They were in different parts of the world, searching, when I gave the radio order for the return to Mars to commence."

Clay considered for a while and then sighed. "I'm afraid you expect an awful lot of me, Kladnor. You belong to a race of skilled scientists, centuries ahead of even the cleverest of our Earth scientists. How do you expect me to do anything when it comes to understanding your powers?"

"You will be taught," Kladnor said patiently. "We have mastered atomic power—by which this ship is driven; we have learned much of other dimensions; we can handle electricity and magnetism and store solar power. We can do almost everything, except give the Princess a flesh-and-blood husband. Synthesis would obviously not do . . . ."

"These Martians . . . ." Clay gazed thoughtfully to-wards the now orange-red speck of Mars. "What are they like ?"

"Being pure inhabitants of their planet they are gro-tesque, from our standards. Possibly eight feet tall, broad-chested. Their height and weight compensates them for Mars' lesser gravity at the surface. We in our underground city have gravity nullifiers which makes the gravity earth-normal. The Martians have always been, and still are, nomadic in the main, though they have one or two towns, too small for detection by Earth telescopes, the principal one being Malacon. In earlier days, when Mars was much like Earth, well watered and vegetated, the Martians did not trouble us—but now the planet is slowly dying, its surface mainly iron-oxide desert and water very scarce except at the Poles, the Martians have become more dangerous. They know we have every needful thing below and it is my belief they plan attack—one day. What they lack in intelligence they make up for in numbers, since they are about a thousand to one against us."

Clay was silent for a long time, turning over the incred-ible events in his mind. Yet they did not seem so incredible any more, so quietly had Kladnor explained every detail. He did not even think it peculiar any more that he was descended from the original Atlanteans. It might explain his love of science, his engineering ability, his liking for being alone with his thoughts without an outsider to disturb him.

"It amounts to one thing," he said at last. "I can either walk into this willingly—or be forced to ?"

"That," Kladnor agreed, "is the issue. Your destiny, Excellency, is to become the husband of Princess Thalia and produce more dignitaries who can carry one where you and the potential Empress will leave off. If you protest I am afraid we shall have to use force. The dignity of the race must be upheld above all things."

Clay smiled a little. "I accept the situation," he said quietly. "And now, if you don't mind, I'd like to freshen up and, if possible, have some different clothes. These climbing togs are hardly the right thing for a . . . dignitary."

Kladnor smiled slightly and motioned. "Come with me, Excellency. ' I will show you your quarters."

CHAPTER TWO.

ARRIVAL ON MARS.

If Clay needed any proof that the Atlanteans hád been sure of their ground in capturing him, he found it in the costume which had been prepared for him. It was an exact fit and of deep orange colour. A bath, in a most superbly fitted chamber with gleaming golden walls, a shave, and the wearing of the costume made Clay feel exactly what he was reputed to be — a dignitary, and the husband-to-be of a Princess.

From this point onwards he found himself looking forward in genuine interest to the hour when he would meet the girl. When he was not sleeping he was studying space, watching the orange-red ball of Mars becoming ever larger. At what speed the space-flyer was moving he had no idea but he judged the velocity to be considerable, for after each rest period Mars had visibly increased in size and Earth, to the rear, had correspondingly become smaller. It was during his studies of the mother planet that Clay saw the seven other golden "saucers" following in the wake of their leader.

"I always thought," Clay said on one occasion as Kladnor stood beside him, "that a space ship ought to look rather like an earthly submarine—pointed at both ends."

Kladnor shrugged. "A space machine can be any design, Excellency, since it has no air resistance to overcome which demands streamlining. We build them this shape for convenience, the storage rooms on the outer rim, connected by tunnels to the controlling rooms and power plant in the hub."

Clay nodded and surveyed the abyss. "How long before we reach Mars ?"

"Possibly three or four days in Earth-time. Since there is no night in space we reckon time by the chronometer."

And, in the main, Kladnor's estimate proved correct. There finally came a time when Mars filled all the void ahead of the space-flyer. Silent, Clay stood at the main outlook window in the huge control room, the rest of the Atlanteans busy at the switchboards making the necessary arrangements for landing the machine safely. It was time which called for concentrated attention on the part of all of them.

For Clay the view was intriguing. Mars' deserts were now absolutely clear, there being no shimmering in the cloudless Martian air. He could see the widely spread squares of cities, presumably belonging to the surface-world Martians, and also the criss-crossing lines stretching across the planet from pole to pole. He hesitated over asking about the much publicised canals, then thought better of it. As commander of the vessel Kladnor had his hands full at the moment giving orders.

As the machine touched the outer edge of the thin Martian atmosphere Clay saw one of the "canals" below suddenly widen to three times its size. He knew in that moment that the so-called waterways were actually the entrance points to the Martian underworld, huge man-made fissures which parted under an order from Kladnor. The greenness about the fissures was evidently caused by vegetation growing in the edges of the enormous valves.

Steadily the flyer dropped down towards the open eye which gaped below. Nearer, and nearer still, to the surface of Mars—and then something happened. From the depths of the gap there suddenly stabbed a pale laveder beam. It struck the vessel on the outer rim, instantly shattering a huge segment so that the machine reeled wildly like a broken wheel.

"It's an attack !" Kladnor exclaimed in amazement, as Clay looked at him in surprise. "Our own weapons are being used against us . . . . "

"The Martians !" Clay said quickly, hurrying over to the switchboard. "There can't be any other explanation."

"But they haven't the intelligence to use our equiment; I'm convinced of it . . . ."

The machine spun crazily in a circle and flung Kladnor, his colleagues, and Clay to the floor.

"Evidently they have !" Clay said grimly, getting up. "It looks as though they've been pretty busy whilst you've been away."

Kladnor struggled to his feet and went to the window. He was just in time to see all hell burst loose from the open eye below—and not only from that one point, either, but from several others. It was more than obvious now that this attack had been withheld until the last moment to secure the advantage of surprise and bring the "saucers" within range.

Amidst a fan of beams the eight machines slewed and rocked crazily, pieces disintegrating from them, spokes buckling, smoke and flame spurting where actual annihilation did not take place. Clay, also watching, saw the machine immediately to the rear suddenly mushroom and split into a thousand pieces, all of which dropped in flaming metal to the ochre wastes below.

"Do we hit back, Kladnor ?" demanded one of the men at the control board, his face strained. "We have the weapons. Shall I . . . ."

"Yes . . yes." Kladnor turned quickly from the window. "Try the heat beams. We may penetrate far enough into the locks to destroy . . . . ."

He had no opportunity to finish his sentence. At that moment the whirling disintegrative beams struck the vessel amidships. There was a whelming roar. Clay spun round in time to see the huge metal stanchions supporting the roof buckling crazily. He flung himself flat but it did not save him from being battered and pounded by falling metal. The whole ship, out of control, was spinning like a top, taking him with it and the Atlanteans who lay crushed under the fallen girders.

Clay had a last vision of Kladnor's dying face, a huge gash across his forehead from which the blood was pouring, then the shattered machine struck the Martian desert with thunderous impact. The shock flung Clay into a pain-ridden darkness from which it seemed eternities before he emerged.

When he did so it was to the contemplation of a high ceiling of the familiar brilliant gold colour. There were sounds around him. He moved to put a hand to his forehead and found he could not. By degrees it dawned on him that he was chained to the wall by wrists and ankles, that he was in a well lighted cell with a metal door, and that the sounds were coming from beyond it.

In the cell there was not a stick of furniture. Only the four polished walls, ceiling, and floor. He moved stiffly, conscious of a dull ache in one arm and at the back of his head.

"Hey!" he called. "Anybody around?"

His cry brought results. There was a sudden clanking outside the door, the sound of a lock turning back, and then a gigantic figure appeared. Dazed, Clay lay and looked at the first true Martian he had ever seen. His skin was a bright green colour and he was a giant, by Earth standards. He was a good eight feet in height with colossal chest and shoulders. His face was not entirely unlike an Earthling's. It was completely hairless, but had a recognisable mouth, nose, and eyes. The eyes were the cruellest Clay had ever seen—round, snakelike, and unblinking, of extremely light colour. For attire the man wore a pair of close fitting shorts, sandals, and a sleeveless affair rather like a leather singlet.

"What's happened?" Clay demanded. "Where am I.?"

From the dumb stare of the cruel eyes he judged that his words had not been understood—as such, but evidently the fact that Clay was alive and moving was sufficient for the guard. He came forward, snapped open the manacles at wrists and ankles, then hauled Clay to his feet with super- lative ease.

Clay did not attempt resistance : he was not such a fool. The enormous muscles on the chest and arms of the guard were proof of his gigantic strength, even without recourse to the queer weapon thrust in the belt of his shorts.

The guard jerked his head to the doorway, so Clay began moving. He found himself in a metal underground corridor, a string of lights stretching along its roof into distance. With the echoes of his own and the guard's foot- steps in his ears he started walking, and kept at it until the passage had been traversed and he stepped out through a gigantic doorway into the main street of a city.

For a moment he stopped, amazed at the vision spread before him. Presumably this was the last city of the Atlan- teans, of which Kladnor had spoken. It had extraordinary beauty with its shining golden metal, well planned streets, terraces, and parks, and here and there a directional power tower spiring up to the cavern roof immensely high overhead. So high indeed that aircraft had room to negotiate the artifi- cial air without danger of collision. Light, as far as Clay could tell, was provided by a synthetic sun hanging mys- teriously unsupported directly over the city, at a height of perhaps five hundred feet. It was warm and brilliant, doubtless supported by magnetism and giving forth the inex- haustible energy of the atom.

Clay absorbed this within a matter of seconds, then he was nudged forward again. He resumed walking, realising as he went that the aches and pains were disappearing and that his interest was sharpening. In particular he noticed that there did not seem to be any Atlanteans in view. The only beings he saw at all in his march to a solitary building apart from the others were Martians, all of them dressed in similar rig to that of his guard. Here and there he glimpsed females, less in height that the men, but apparently immensely strong. They too were green, but of a lighter shade than the males, and had the same cold, unwinking eyes that had something in common with a tiger.

So, presently, Clay entered the isolated building, passed through a broad hall lined with Martian guards, and then evidently into a council chamber. A solitary Martian was within, seated at a desk. In fact the whole setup reminded Clay of the chamber he had entered aboard the flying saucer when he had first met Kladnor.

But here there was no kindly-faced man with wisdom in his features—only a creature with a merciless jaw and boring eyes whose snakelike stare was almost hypnotic.

"So you are Clayton Drew," the creature said, after he had dismissed the guard.

"Yes." Clay did not attempt to be respectful. The very sight of the man stirred inner hostility.

"You can thank us for your recovery," the Martian added, in his thick, heavy voice. "It was not done because we have any particular love for you, Earthman, but because we need you."

"You too ?" Clay asked dryly. "First it was Kladnor; now it is you. I seem to be a mighty important person as far as this planet is concerned."

"A specimen of rarity such as yourself is important," the Martian agreed cynically. Then he got to his feet, a massively powerful being in his light blue singlet and shorts. "I am Lexas," he said. "I have become ruler during the absence of the Atlantean intelligentsia. I have waited all my life for this to happen, just as my ancestors waited before me. I am a rightful inhabitant of this planet; the people of Atlantis were not."

"Were not ?" Clay repeated, watching the giant narrowly.

"Only a handful are left," Lexas explained. "A few who can teach us scientific tricks—as they fired weapons at our command. Then there is . . . the Princess Thalia."

"Where is she ?" Clay demanded, and wondered vaguely why he felt so concerned over the safety of a girl he had never seen.

"Safely imprisoned at the moment, in Malacon. Her rule is ended ; mine has taken its place. Fortunate, is it not, that I have mastered your language, Earthman ? I did it especially so that I could converse with you. I heard from the Atlanteans left behind here that you were coming."

"All right, so I'm here," Clay said. "Now what happens ? I suppose you have the same idea as Kladnor had—that I marry the Princess Thalia ?

"No." The big mouth of the Martian split into a grin. His teeth were fanged and double-rowed. "Our aim, Earthman, is to destroy the Atlantean race completely, not perpetuate it. You are here as a speciment of Earth-male. It is our wish to find out exactly how you are constituted."

If Clay felt any sudden chill of fear at the observation he did not show it. The Martian eyed him fixedly and then added, "Just as the Princess Thalia is a good female subject. She is remotely descended from Earth and, as such, is moulded in Earth-form . . . . As male specimens we *could* have used one or other of the Atlantean men, of course, but why should we do that when we can have a man who is direct from Earth, and not refined by untold generations of culture on this planet."

Lexas had been pacing about whilst speaking. Now he came to a stop beside the desk and gave Clay a questioning look.

"You take it quietly, Earthman."

"I'm trying to weigh things up," Clay answered, which was more than the literal truth. "Why exactly should you want a male and female specimen of Earth physique ?"

"Is it not obvious, Earthman ? We of Mars, as you call our planet, are surface creatures. We cannot live comfortably on the surface of our world any longer. Hence our invasion of this underworld the moment the chance was opportune. But now we find we cannot live down here, either : it is foreign to our natures and the artificial gravitation is a deadly drag upon us. We are used to much less attraction on the surface. These Atlantean fools are too stubborn to cut off the nullifier machines, so we are compelled to endure the burden of heavy gravity . . . To all this there is only one answer—We must find a world where we can live on the surface, in comfort."

"Meaning Earth ?" Clay asked deliberately.

The Martian nodded his great bald head.

"Exactly. But to go to Earth as we are now would be no benefit. That is why we must determine the structure of an Earth man and woman so we can make ourselves like them."

"And how do you suppose you can do that ?"

"The surgery of Atlantis is far reaching, my friend. We can make synthetic beings identical to yourself and the Princess and then have our brains transplanted into those bodies. It can be done by mechanical means, once we have forced the remaining Atlantean technicians to explain away their secrets. After that, conquest of your world would be simple . . . . . A vast armada of flying-saucers—as you poetically call them—would descend on your world, and subdue its peoples."

That the danger was very real, Clay had no doubts—but he was also thinking of other things the Martian had said. One was that the Princess Thalia was in Malacon, one of the surface cities—according to Kladnor ; the other was that the gravity in the underworld was scientifically controlled. Finally, there was the fact that a few Atlantean scientists were still alive, though probably under heavy guard.

It meant either action, and perhaps death as the reward ; or death anyway and no action at all. Clay came to a decision in a matter of moments and asked a question.

"In this analysis of living bodies you speak of, Lexas, do they have to be living ?"

The Martian was taken off his guard. "Of course. A dead body without functions would not tell us anything."

Clay grinned. "Then it won't pay you to kill me off in a hurry, so I might as well try a few tricks of my own."

His sentence .was hardly finished before he catapulted himself forward in a tackle and gripped the Martian round his massive shins. The terrific wrench Clay gave toppled the giant over on his back. A volley of words in his own language escaped him, then they stopped abruptly as a smashing blow in the jaw slammed his head back on the polished floor. He heaved and writhed, but in those few seconds his weapon had gone from his belt and Clay held it steadily—even though he had not yet figured out how to use it.

"This will be quite useful to me, Lexas," he said, his eyes glinting. "You've got size, I know, but the heavy gravity down here hampers you. Sit down at your desk!"

Sullenly, watching his chance to hit back, the Martian usurper did as ordered. Clay glanced about, then backed away, still keeping Lexas covered with the weapon, until he had arrived at one of the ornamental hassocks. With his free hand he ripped away the fancy cords bound about it and returned with them. Tossing a loop into one of them he drew it taut about the Martian's sinewy neck and then secured it to the back of the chair. After that it did not take long to bind the Martian's wrists and ankles.

"By all normal standards I ought to kill you," Clay said, looking at the Martian's furious face as the cord held his neck tautly. "Funny thing, I've an aversion to killing anything—even a Martian—unless it's only me or him for it. At the moment you've escaped with your life, but don't trespass too far on my good nature."

"You insane, Earth fool!" Lexas panted, striving with his huge strength to break free. "How far do you think this will get you?"

"That's my business. Let me tell you something Lexas. : . . . ." Clay went close enough for the weapon's barrel to press on the Martian's temple—and the way he cringed proved it was loaded. "I was made Emperor-designate of Mars before I landed on this hell-fired planet. Kladnor did that, one of the highest of the Atlantean dignitaries. We made a bargain, you understand? I agreed to his con-

ditions—namely, to marry the Princess Thalia and perpetuate
the Atlantean race, because I myself am a descendant of
Atlantis. And that is exactly what I intend to do, and if I
can blow your rotten heirarchy to blazes in the doing I'll do
it !"

With that Clay tugged off the sash he was still wearing
about his Atlantean tunic and drew it taut across the Martian's mouth, smothering the words he was about to utter.

"That should fix you for a bit," Clay murmured, then
he sped towards the doorway. Here he paused, studied his
weapon for a moment to decide how it worked—apparently
from a button switch—and then opened the door cautiously
and peering into the hig hall. At a distance of fifty yards the
guards were lined up, motionless, but ready for action.

Clay promptly withdrew again and hurried across to
the window. It opened at a touch and gave on to a wide
courtyard. Clay slid over the windowledge, hung by his
hands for a moment, and then dropped lightly. Instantly
he had his weapon out of his belt again in readiness.

The courtyard was deserted, and there was a gate at
the end of it. Clay did not immediately go towards it. He
kept flat against the wall beside which he had dropped, so
the windows overlooking the courtyard were not in line with
him. From here he studied the skyline of the city. His
immediate need was to somehow contact an Atlantean engineer—a friend—who would be able to help, and to his way of
thinking, the most likely place to find one was in one of
the power houses since, from what Lexas had said, it seemed
that as yet only the Atlanteans knew how to control the city's
essential services.

Finally Clay's gaze settled on one of the nearer power
towers springing some three hundred feet upwards towards
the cavern roof. At the base of it there must surely be a building where an Atlantean, or group of them, would be working.

Clay began moving swiftly, still keeping close in to the
wall. He would have been thankful for the cover of darkness but, as he knew, that would never come. The atomic

ball overhead glowed incessently and cast forth its pouring golden light and beating heat.

Outside the courtyard gate Clay hesitated. There was a main road which apparently went into the heart of the city—and in the direction of the nearest power tower. At the moment there were no Martians about—only queerly designed vehicles moving at high speed. He kept just behind the gate's main pillar and watched the traffic for a while—and then it occurred to him that this was a traffic-level only. There was no provision for pedestrians.

· "Only one way," he muttered, examining his gun—then he held it in readiness for when the next vehicle should come into view.

His wait was not a long one. Very soon, one of the bullet-nosed cars, probably powered by atomic force and completely silent, came speeding into sight. Clay waited until it was fairly close and then stepped from concealment boldly with his weapon levelled.

In fact he was too bold, for a moment after he had pointed his weapon a stream of murderous fire jetted at him from a concealed point low down on the vehicle. Evidently he was considered to be an Atlantean, both in physique and attire, which was sufficient reason for trying to wipe him out. But fortunately for him the speed of the vehicle made the driver's aim bad and the murderous beam missed him by inches.

He retaliated instantly, and was appalled for a moment at the frightful power of the thing he had in his hand. A beam as blue as sapphire shot like a needle from the gunmouth and blasted clean through the protective glass round the driver. It was dead on the mark. The driver's head disappeared in a sudden whoosh of flame and belching smoke.

In this space of time the vehicle had swept on for fifty yards. Now it skidded crazily, turned a complete semi-circle whilst still on its wheels, and then crashed into the metal railings at the side of the road. It came to a stop, its engine still humming and evidently out of gear.

Clay looked about him quickly. No other vehicles were coming along the broad, lengthy track at the moment. He raced to the vehicle and dragged open the half shattered door. The decapitated body of the Martian fell out. Clay seized it under the armpits and dragged it to the railings, looking over them into an abyss such as he had never expected to find. This particular traffic-level, it appeared, was perched some two hundred feet over the lower bowels of the cavern.

With an effort he lifted up the corpse, rested it on the rail for a second or two, and then heaved. Grim-faced, he watched it go hurtling down into the depths, arms and legs flying. It struck bottom soundlessly, amidst what was apparently disused mine workings—probably dating back to the time when the Atlanteans had withdrawn Mars' more valuable ores. Just what would be thought when the headless Martian was found Clay did not know — nor care, at the moment.

He turned, then started. In the distance another vehicle was approaching. As yet it was only a speck, but moving at a terrific speed.

In one dive he gained the vehicle the Martian had been driving and clambered into the control seat, shutting the damaged door as best he could. The inside of the "car" smelled of burned flesh and fumes. The dashboard was complicated beyond anything Clay had imagined. To the rear of him were two more empty seats.

He listened for a moment or two to the throbbing of the engine and wondered what the hell he should do next. The thing he feared most was that the oncoming driver would stop and ask if he needed help. He glanced in the twin reflecting mirrors and saw the other vehicle approaching swiftly—then one of the many buttons he was jabbing frantically suddenly did something. With a terrific surge of power he swept clean across the traffic level, broadside, the nose of the vehicle ramming the oncoming car with blinding impact.

Clay was flung back violently in his seat, his head sing-
ing with the concussion. Apparently his own vehicle was not
very much damaged—but the other one, caught clean in the
centre, was flung over and over. It hit the railings, poised
for a ghastly second, then in a snapping of metal bars it over-
balanced and vanished through the gap. The noise it made
as it hit the rock below was distinct to Clay even in the
enclosed cabin.

He gulped to himself, pressed that devilish button again,
and once more the thing started flying forward at such a
speed he thought he would become airborne. Then he found
the steering X—or that was how it looked to him. Two bars
of metal in X-design which controlled the left-right movement
of the front wheels. Next he discovered a notched bar which
highered or lowered his speed. He cut down to half and felt
perspiration pouring down his face.

Of one thing he was certain. This was not an ordinary
power-driven vehicle. It absorbed its motive force from
somewhere and just kept on going, perhaps eternally, only
moving when the engine was put in gear. Then he remem-
bered something Kladnor had said about stored solar energy.
Perhaps that was it.

Just at the moment he had no time to work out engineering principles. His whole being was concentrated on controlling his crazy chariot as he hurtled it at close on seventy
miles an hour down the traffic level. He could see that in
the distance the level opened out into the thick of the town
itself, and that there were vehicles moving across intersec-
tions. His heart began to race as he wondered what he would
do when he got there. If he got there. His main ambition
was to reach that power tower which was now on his right.

He thought swiftly as he hurtled along, then presently
he made up his mind. Stopping the vehicle abruptly by
snapping up the control button he jumped out and raced to
the side of the level, looking over it. Here there were no
yawning depths, only rock plain extending away from the
level and out into distance where stood the power tower he

wanted.

"Worth a try," he muttered, and hurried back to the machine.

Jumping in, he started it forward, then slewed it round and drove with all the power he could gather straight at the metal railings. The machine jolted and bounced under the shock, but it got through with sheer speed and strong construction. Like a tank it went jolting over the rocks, pitching Clay helplessly up and down in his seat so that his head kept hitting the roof with painful concussions.

But the building at the base of the tall tower was coming nearer, and that was the main thing. He tugged his gun from his belt, and then thought again. The vehicle itself, as he had good reason to know, had a concealed weapon of its own. But exactly where ? He began to fiddle again with the various switches on the control board as he kept one hand on the X-bars. And he found what he wanted a little bit too thoroughly. Quite unexpectedly, as a switch closed under his hand, that sapphire beam stabbed forth from the vehicle's front. It struck the side of the building, fused the metal as though it were butter, and passed beyond. What happened then Clay was not sure.

There was some kind of explosion, terrific in its force. The whole building lifted right out of its rock base and flew into the air in a mass of crumbling pieces. With the debris went a mushroom of smoke which could only mean an atomic pile had been touched off somewhere.

But this was not all. Darkness descended suddenly—far too suddenly for Clay's liking. Not expecting it he had driven his vehicle into the midst of twisted metal and flickering flame before he knew what had happened. The vehicle came to grinding halt, its nose hard against a mighty girder. Blinking at an incandescent glare of fire, against which one figure was moving slowly and painfully, Clay crawled out of the cab and looked about him.

Everywhere in the distance alarm bells seemed to be ringing. The darkness where the city stood was appalling,

the darkness such as only the depths can produce. But just
here it was bright enough, so Clay moved forward, gun in
hand, and for a moment watched the figure which was reeling
towards him. When he saw it was no taller than himself
he went forward.

' He came face to face with the man in a moment or two.
His tunic was scorched, blood streaked across his face and
hands, but at least he was alive and not a Martian.

"Can you speak English ? Earth language ?" Clay
demanded, gripping the man's arm.

"We all can," he answered, dazed. "You with the rest
of us. Did not her Highness make us learn it ?"

"Very sensible of her," Clay said. "How badly are you
hurt ?"

"Cuts . . . bad bruises. Burns." The man gasped for
breath. "I'll be all right. I . . . I must rest a moment."

He sank down on the rocks and for a while gazed fixedly
at the slowly decreasing glare in the ruins of the power-
house.

"What happened ?" Clay asked, surveying the deepen-
ing dark.

"I don't quite know. Something disintegrative struck
the heart of the power-plant and of course, since the plant is
atomic, that meant an inconceivably violent explosion. It
did me a good turn, though. I was working under orders,
guarded by two Martians. They were blown to pieces. I
got flung flat and escaped the worst . . . .".

"Good," Clay muttered. "I'd better explain who I am.
I'm the Emperor-designate—Clay Drew of Earth, and descendant of Hertis."

"You are ?"   There was a sudden reverence in the
man's tone and he peered at Clay intently in the flickering
light. "So that is why I did not recognise you. Your Excellency," he went on hurriedly, "I beg of you to forgive
my . . . . ."

"Forgive nothing, my friend," Clay answered. "I blew
up the power house by accident, and I seem to have done

it properly. But just why is everything in the dark ?"

"Because you have destroyed the power in one of the four towers responsible for our synthetic sun. It was composed of atomic energy in a state of balance, these towers being used both to feed it and keep it poised in mid-air."

"Suits me fine," Clay murmured. "How long will it take to put it right ?"

"Twelve hours maybe, granting the technicians will do it. What few there are of us left don't exactly enjoy obeying the orders of the Martians . . . ." The Atlantean paused for a moment as the last traces of fire died out of the shattered power-house, then he looked towards the distant city as light came into being again, but this time it was on the ground, shining in strings along the streets, winking in the windows of the edifices.

"I'm concerned with only one thing," Clay said after a moment. "I want to locate the Princess Thalia, make sure she is safe, and find some means of kicking these Martian lowbrows out on their ears. In fact I mean to destroy them, before they destroy us and the world from which I've come."

"So their ambitions extend that far ?" the technician asked.

"Lexas himself told me as much. I got away from him." Clay looked at the emergency lighting of the distant city and then added, "This darkness is the one thing I want. I can move fast, but I need help. How do I get to the surface of this planet ?"

"Only by the shafts. I can show you, but it won't do any good. The shafts are controlled from switchboards in a special building and the Martians know how to run them. Nothing complicated there for them to understand."

"The fact remains I have got to reach Malacon, where the Princess is imprisoned." Clay gripped the man's arm. "Don't you realise the situation, man ? We've got to fight, pull every trick we know, otherwise these Martians will have us licked. At the moment we have a head start, and I'm asking for your help. If that doesn't work, then I demand it, as a dignitary."

"As you wish, Excellency," the man responded. "I was only thinking of the risks."

"What is your name ?" Clay asked him.

"Clafnel. I'm a leading atomic engineer."

"That may be useful later. Tell me something, Clafnel. The gravity inside here is artificially created, I believe. Is it possible to increase or decrease its power at will ?"

"If necessary, yes. It can produce the strains one would expect on mighty Jupiter, or the lightness of Mercury. Why do you ask, Excellency ?"

"Just a thought I have. How do we get to the place where the gravity is controlled ?"

"The building is some two miles from here, on the edge of the city. Men of our own kind are in control, but watched over by Martians as I was."

"That's where we're heading for to begin with," Clay decided, getting to his feet. "That is, if you are fit for such an excursion ?"

"I would prefer to return to my home first for ointments and balms," Clafnel replied, also rising. "These burns are painful. Further, I need a weapon, such as you have. We can get provisions, rest awhile if need be . . . ."

"Good enough," Clay interrupted. "Whereabouts is your home ? Can we reach it in safety ?"

"In this darkness, yes. It's on the outskirts of the city —And we'd better move quickly," Clafnel added, with a glance about him. "At any time now this tower explosion may be investigated. We can use your solar-car."

"So it does use the power of sun ?" Clay asked, moving towards the vehicle in the darkness. "I rather wondered about that."

"The power is distributed through the underworld in the form of radiation-waves," Clafnel explained, as he and Clay climbed into the driving cabin. "The motor simply picks up the power as a radio receiver picks up transmission."

Clay nodded, pressed the motor button, and then set the

vehicle bumping and bounding over the rockery. Clafnel
pressed another switch and a powerful headlight beamed
ahead, illuminating the rocky landscape.

"Good job the Martians have taken a long time investi-
gating that tower," Clay said presently.

"Probably because they don't know for certain yet what
has happened; our science still baffles them, remember. They
think they can learn it by abuse and threats, but they have
yet to discover how tough we Atlanteans can be when it comes
to revealing the secrets of generations."

"How many of you are there left ?" Clay questioned.
"Lexas said a 'handful'."

"About two hundred men and women," Clafnel responded, his eyes watching the rocky terrain intently. "Bear
left !" he instructed suddenly, and Clay obeyed.

So, by degrees, they came nearer and nearer to the
lights of the city, following the rocky plain which extended
outside it. Acting under Clafnel's orders Clay came at last
to a block of low-roofed buildings, each with identical doors, a street passing along in front of them. At the
moment the vista was empty save for the solar-car and the
two men inside it. The lighting was somewhat dim, from
overhead lamps, but clear enough to see by.

"We can't remain long undisturbed," Clafnel said:
"That's my home there"—and he pointed to the middle doorway with a number 6 upon it. "The trouble is this solar-car
may give us away."

Clay looked about him, then presently his gaze centred
on a grating of considerable size further up the street. He
gave an enquiring glance.

"Sewer inspection cover," Clafnel said.

"And big enough to take this bus," Clay decided. "All
I need to know. Give me a hand to get the grid up."

Clay did not wait to be handed an argument. He climbed
out of the vehicle and hurried over to the grid, locking his
fingers in the bars. Single-handed he could not have accom-
plished anything, but with the assistance of Clafnel he suc-

ceeded in raising the grating on its well-oiled hinges and laying it back flat on to the road.

"Okay—all I want," Clay said, and raced back to the vehicle. "Pity to lose our one means of fast locomotion but it's better than being nabbed."

He leaned inside the driving cabin, fixed the X-bars so the front wheels were straight, and then switched on at low speed. The vehicle began moving, gathering impetus, then when it reached the gaping hole in the street it toppled over the rim and crashed with a clangour of metal into the depths. To close the grid down again was only the work of a few moments.

"You are very wholesale in your methods, Excellency," Clafnel remarked, looking bewildered.

"Nothing else for it in a setup like this. Now let's get into your place ; it'll be safer."

Clafnel nodded and began moving. When he reached the door of his home he operated a lock which seemed to be of the combination type and the door opened silently. In another moment he and Clay were in a dark hall.

"A moment, Excellency," Clafnel murmured. "I will close over the shutters before putting on the emergency lights."

"You have shutters then ? Why, in a place where sunlight is normally here all the twenty four hours ?"

"So that we can sleep in any room, in darkness. That is a natural desire."

Clafnel moved away in the blackness and Clay heard the sound of shutters being closed ; then soft lighting sprang into being in a room off the hall. He advanced into it and looked about him upon comfortable furniture. It would have been hard to think that the room was on Mars, 40-million miles from Earth, so normal was it. Yet, since the people of Atlantis had originally sprung from Earth there was perhaps nothing so very remarkable about it.

"If you will make youself comfortable, Excellency," Clafnel invited, with a motion of his hand. "I will just attend to my wounds and then bring in some refreshment."

He hurried away and Clay settled down in one of the softly sprung chairs. Before many minutes had passed Clafnel returned, ointment gleaming on his burns and cuts, the dirt removed from his handsome features. In his hands was a tray loaded with concentrates and the familiar yellow wine.

"Humble fare, your Excellency," Clafnel apologised. "I have done my best."

"No man can do more," Clay shrugged. "And incidentally, since we are likely to be together quite a lot from here on, you can drop the title. At present I am not a dignitary—I only hope to become one. So call me Clay."

"As you order—Clay." And Clafnel poured out the wine and then handed over the concentrates.

Chapter Three.

ESCAPE !

In spite of their good intentions to get on the move immediately they had rested, Clay and the Atlantean found that Nature had a stronger claim. They both fell asleep in their chairs and only awoke again to a thunderous hammering on the main outer door of the dwelling.

Clafnel was the first to fully recover his wits. He got to his feet quickly and sped to the bureau-like piece of furniture in the corner. From it he took a weapon similar to Clay's and held it steadily.

"Apparently we've been followed, Clay," he said, as Clay rose and withdrew his own weapon in readiness from his belt.

"Don't see how they could, in the dark."

"Radio detection, Excellency. We were driving a vehicle which betrays its presence by the solar-emanations it gives off. The Martians themselves are not clever enough to read the instruments, but evidently they forced our comrades to do it for them."

The hammering continued and presently a voice boomed forth, speaking in a strange language. Clafnel's face was grim as he listened.

"Martian guards," he said. "They say they know we're in here and order us to open the door, otherwise they'll blow this domicile, and the others, to pieces."

"They won't," Clay said confidently. "They wouldn't

stop at destroying you, I don't suppose, but it's different with me. I happen to be very valuable. It's only because I'm here that they haven't blown the place up already. Why knock and tell us they're going to do it?"

"We might try and get out," Clafnel said quickly. "There is a back entrance, but I expect it will be guarded."

He hurried to the table, scooped into his pockets all the concentrates he could collect, and then motioned Clay out of the room. In the darkness they went along a narrow passage and Clafnel fumbled with a lock at the end of it. He opened the door slowly, and instantly a blaze of light flooded into his face from a torch held by a Martian outside.

Clafnel fell back, trying to close the door—but Clay was not so hesitant. He pushed the door wider, brought up his gun, and fired relentlessly. The sapphire needle evidently struck home for there was a scream of anguish and the torch waved wildly and then dropped.

"Quick!" Clay snapped, gripping Clafnel's arm. "Outside! And don't argue with these brutes—Wipe 'em out!"

He lunged down the steps and came up against two more gigantic forms dimly visible against the light from the street at the front of the building. He tried to fire but his gun arm was deflected, so he landed a hammer punch straight in front of him, and back of it was all the power of his well-developed muscles.

Being so tall the Martian got the piston impact straight in the stomach. Winded, he doubled up; then he groaned and dropped as the beam of Clafnel's gun struck clean through his skull.

The second Martian flung himself forward, intending to deal with both men at once—and evidently his orders were not to kill for he did not use his weapon. Which was just too bad for him. Clay fired without mercy, twice, and brought the giant down in smoking, dying anguish to the ground.

"Let's get out," Clay said briefly. "There are others at the front, remember."

Clafnel nodded and led the way across a small enclosed
space, and so through a gate which the Martians had already
opened. In a moment or two he and Clay were in a narrow
street where only one solitary lamp illuminated their movements.

"This way," the technician said. "It'll be safer to move
over the roofs of the town."

He hurried through the dim light to a very earthly-
looking fire escape fastened to the side of an edifice and began
to climb the rungs swiftly with Clay behind him. In a matter
of perhaps three minutes they had reached the flat roof. Clay
looked about him, breathing hard.

From here the whole of the city with its lighted streets
and windows was spread out before him, a wilderness of roofs
and high and low buildings, all gleaming with the sheen of
gold—and over it was the utter blackness of the cavern roof.
There was noise too—the sound of powerful vehicles on the
move, the drone of aircraft, and the throbbing of energy
from the various nerve-centres of the city.

"That's the building we want," Clafnel said, and pointed
over the roof parapet to an edifice about half a mile away,
distinguishable by the queer blunt-nosed tower it projected
into the air.

"That thing a magnet?" Clay asked.

"Magnetic principle," Clafnel assented. "It is used for
absorbing the energy of the sun through the rock between
us and the surface—X-ray fashion—And they're after us!"
he added in sudden urgency, as there came shouts from the
narrow street below.

Clay darted forward quickly across the roof, reached the
parapet and then measured his distance to the next—and
lower—roof. He poised, crouched, and then flung himself
into space with all his strength. He crossed the gap of street
between the buildings with only a few inches to spare—and
kept on running forward. Clafnel followed immediately
behind him.

They found the next jump easier, but the one after that

was greater than Clay had suspected. He fell short and flung out his hands desperately, only just catching his fingers on the parapet and swinging dizzily in space.

He glanced below at the street, fifty feet down. Traffic was moving ; people were going back and forth, most of them Martians as far as he could tell in the dim light. Then he began to try and muscle himself upwards. His first effort failed, which made it all the harder for his second attempt.

"Hurry up, Clay, for heaven's sake !" came the voice of Clafnel on the roof behind him. "I can't leap until you're clear. You're in my way."

Clay made another effort and strained his arms to the uttermost. He got his chin as high as the parapet but that was the limit. Gradually he sank back again, his feet kicking, perspiration streaming down his face.

"I would suggest you do not waste any further time, Earthman," a voice said from the roof behind him, and then a curt order was added. "Get him, you men."

Clay could not turn and look but he knew well enough that for the moment his escape was stopped. He could feel his fingers slipping gradually under his weight—then one of the long-legged Martians had leapt across the gap, missing him by a fraction. In another moment Clay felt the powerful hands seizing him and he was dragged upwards. As he was dumped on the flat roof the idea of resistance passed through his mind and then died. He just hadn't the strength, and in any case the guard had his gun ready.

Slowly Clay got to his feet and found his weapon snatched from his belt. He turned and looked across the gap to where Clafnel was firmly held in the midst of three guards. A little apart from them was yet another Martian, and his coarse voice immediately identified him. As Clay had suspected, from the Martian's earlier remarks, it was Lexas himself.

"You would do well to realise, Earthman, that escape is not practicable," he said. "I have sent one of my men for a grapple ladder. When he returns you will join us."

Clay did not say anything. Clafnel, he realised, was hopelessly caught, and would probably forfeit his life, but on this side of the street there was only the one Martian, now standing at the rear. Clay half smiled to himself in the dim light. He was reasonably sure that he would not be shot at whilst chase could be given . . . .

"You gave me a long pursuit, Earthman," Lexas called. "I intend to repay you for it, and for the men of my race you have killed and the machinery you have destroyed. . . ."

Clay acted. Abruptly he dropped on his knees. The Martian to his rear, suspecting trickery, bent down to see what was happening, and at that instant Clay stood up again, bracing himself for shock. The top of his skull cracked violently under the Martian's jaw. Then Clay swung round, catching the giant off balance. He lashed out his right with all the power of his arm, sending the giant tottering, the blow taking him just above the heart.

Diving, Clay used his tackle methods—again successfully. The man was flung from his feet and in coming down caught the back of his head against the parapet with sufficient force to give forth a click. Stunned, perhaps killed—Clay was at no trouble to discover which—the Martian relaxed.

"Get him !" Lexas shouted hoarsely, realising what had happened, but by that time Clay was on his way, his own and the Martian's gun tucked in his belt.

Lexas fumed and raved in his own language as his men hesitated at making the dangerous jump, and up to now the guard with the grapple ladder had not arrived . . . . Clay moved fast, vaulted from the roof where he had left the Martian, and dropped in a dizzying rush to the next lower building.

Breathless, he kept going, getting further and further away from the frantic shouts of Lexas, and since nobody knew his destination—except Clafnel, who would never speak—Clay was satisfied that advance warning could not be sent.

Roof after roof he crossed, sometimes helped by overhead

wiring bridging the streets. Gradually he came nearer to the edifice with the blunt-nosed tower, and in a final flying leap he reached it, stumbled, and recovered his balance. He glanced about him, both his guns ready. Nobody was in sight on the broad flat expanse so he hurried to the trap which lay closed some little distance away. Opening it gently he peered below upon a wilderness of scientific machinery. Hot air came gushing up into his face, filled with the reek of oil.

Intently he surveyed the movement of oil-filmed pistons, whirling cogs, glittering tubes of electric energy, everything lighted by brilliant shadowless globes. There were aisles between the machines and along the nearest one to the trap there presently appeared two Martians, guns in their belts, talking to each other as they evidently performed routine sentry duty.

Clay grinned harshly to himself and levelled his right-hand gun, waiting until the men came within the sight on the end of the barrel. He gave them no warning, no chance to draw. He had already learned that on this planet he had to shoot first and ask questions afterwards if he was ever to get results.

The sapphire beam stabbed suddenly as he pressed the button. The right hand Martian blew to pieces instantly, all the water in his body vaporised. His companion glanced up in alarm, dropped his hand to his own weapon, and then crashed face down on the aisle with a gaping hole torn straight through his chest.

Clay waited a moment or two to see what happened. He soon discovered. Two Atlantean technicians came speeding into view. They stopped at the sight of the fallen Martians and looked about them—then upwards as Clay called to them.

"How many more of these gentlemen are there ?" he demanded. "In this building, I mean."

"None—they were quite enough," one man answered feelingly. "Who are you ?"

"I'll explain that in a moment . . . ." And Clay levered himself through the gap, caught at the nearest roof stanchion, then began to slide his way down. In perhaps three minutes he had reached the floor and hurried across to the two astonished men.

"You're dressed like one of us, and you're the same in dimensions," the second man said, in wonder, "but who are . . . . ."

"I'm Clay Drew, of Earth, and I haven't much time." Nevertheless Clay took long enough to explain the situation to date and then concluded, "I'm here to alter the gravitation machines. If we can only increase the gravitational load by about seventy five per cent these Martians will be rooted to the floor. Even as it is, accustomed to the light gravity of the surface, they have a struggle to get about."

"With a seventy five per cent increase we too will be in difficulties," one of the technicians pointed out. "We shall not be able to move properly."

"Anyway, try it," Clay ordered, and because he was a dignitary the men did not even hesitate. He followed them along the aisle and to a massive switchboard with a chair screwed before it. Here, to judge from the multitudes of dials and meters, the entire system of artificial gravity was controlled.

"Hurry it up, Clay insisted. "They're liable to catch up with me at any moment."

One of the men nodded and settled in the chair. He started to turn a graded pointer and the rhythm of the various engines began to alter, becoming deeper and more resonant. Clay could feel the effect almost immediately—a curious dragging-down of his internal organs and the feeling that his limbs were having lead weights put upon them . . . .

Then as a sapphire beam suddenly flashed across his vision and blasted a hole clean through the seated technician's back he realised that Lexas had arrived, and evidently entered silently.

He twirled round, firing his gun. He just missed the

Martian who was crouching behind a nearby machine. The man at Clay's side started to run—his only means of perhaps saving himself since he had no weapon—but it did not avail him anything. He was shot down relentlessly and crashed over on to his face.

The man in the control chair slumped sideways, his hand still holding the power control even in death. But as he fell something happened. The lever was moved across to the lower notches and Clay felt the lead weights fall away from him. Instead he felt incredibly buoyant. Only when the droning of the engines came to a stop did he understand what had happened. The artificial gravity had been cut off altogether and there remained only the natural pull of Mars, about a quarter less than that of Earth.

The issue had been settled for him, and he was not at all sure but what the accident was not a happy one. It made the Martians comfortable, certainly, so that they could move about with ease—four of them were standing watching him now with their guns ready, Lexas immediately to their rear apparently deciding what to do next—but it gave Clay super-human powers.

Suddenly he leapt, and put all his muscular strength into the effort. He succeeded beyond his wildest expectation. No Earth pole vaulter could have equalled the magnificent thirty foot jump he made from a standing position, sailing quite ten feet over the heads of the astounded Martians. His plan to ground them by excess gravity having failed Clay had only one course to follow—get out, and quickly.

His second leap carried him over a group of silent machines and to the door. By this time Lexas and his men had realised what had happened and were charging after him. That they could have shot him down Clay new full well, but evidently they still preferred his living body—for vivisection and study—to his corpse. Therein lay his chance.

He reached the door, whirled it open, and slammed it behind him. There was no lock on the outside with which to secure it, so he kept on going. More Martians were in the corridor, perhaps six of them. Leaving their guns in their belts they moved forward to bar his progress. He kept on running at them until he was three feet away, then again he leapt and sailed over their heads like a man in a slow motion film.

More by luck than anything he found the main doorway and hurtled through it into the street. Moving at a terrific speed thanks to the lightness of his body he twisted and turned in and out of the traffic, finally got across the street, and then raced in ten league strides down a vista which might lead to anywhere for all he knew. As yet there was no pursuit, and he was pretty certain that there would be none, either. Lost in the midst of the city he would not be easy to find.

Now and again a Martian man or woman appeared. He no longer had any need to draw his gun. He simply hurtled over the obstacle and kept on going—exactly where he did not know. Just as long as he put as much distance as possible between himself and Lexas.

Then as he gradually came beyond the confines of the city and into the gloom of the surrounding rocky country he began to take stock of his situation. His plan to chain the Martians to the ground by sheer gravity had fallen through. It was reasonably certain now that the gravity would stay as Martian normal since the Martians had discovered, by the death of the technician, just how the power was controlled, something which had formerly escaped them.

And, if the gravity did stay as slight as it was now, it opened up possibilities. Clay summed them up as he walked along with feather-lightness amidst the rocks. He would be able to leap prodigous distances, able to climb difficult heights with hardly any weight to drag him back—That was it ! To find a shaft to the surface and escape. The Princess Thalia was his objective. Once he had located her, removed her from imprisonment in Malacon, he might return with a new plan to destroy the interlopers in the underground.

He stopped, looking about him. Clafnel, unfortunately,

had not told him where the shafts were located, had merely said that they were controlled from a special building. Clay sat down and rested for a while, his face grim at the thought of having to engage in yet another struggle in one of the edifices. This time, if Lexas caught up with him, all orders not to kill might go by the board. It was hardly likely the Martian ruler's temper had been improved by the slippery escapes of his enemy. .

As he pondered Clay found himself looking at the aircraft speeding by high in the cavern roof. They were not passing over him—in fact they were quite a mile away—engaged on different errands, their lights gleaming now that the artificial sun had been destroyed. But the point that presently interested Clay was that not all of them headed towards the city, there to land. Some of them went spiralling upwards into the dark of the cavern roof and were mysteriously lost to sight.

"That's it !" he breathed, snapping his fingers. "They're not just cruising around in this colossal cavern ; they're travelling to the exterior. Maybe bringing in stuff from the surface towns for use by the Martians."

His explanation was probably logical enough. Whether it was or not did not concern him ; he was preoccupied with the problem of how to get aboard one of the machines and be carried up the unseen shaft to the surface. Evidently several of them were permanently open to give the aircraft free passage.

Finally he made up his mind. Many of the planes seemed to cross a point some distance away where the rock ground rose sharply into a small hill—some kind of massive spur which had evidently never been levelled out. Clay began heading towards it, secure in the darkness and hoping that the sun—or a new one—would not be re-kindled. Perhaps the technicians would prove too difficult to persuade.

In ten minutes, moving at his usual tremendous pace, Clay had reached the rising ground. He went up the rocky incline in big leaps, gaining the summit—perhaps a hundred feet above the general level of rock—some little time later. Here he sat down and kept himself concealed by smaller spurs as much as possible until a plane came along.

As he had suspected, the machine—completely silent and shaped like a bullet—swept over his head. Perhaps, even, the rock was some kind of marker, as a lighthouse might be to a ship. Whatever the cause every machine crossed it at about a twenty foot height. This fact decided, Clay began experimenting with the limit of his jumping powers until he felt he might make an attempt.

The next time a plane approached he studied it intently, trying to discover in the dimly reflected lights of the city, and glow from the lamps on the machine itself, if there was an undercarriage. Apparently there was not—or if there was it had been retracted. Which made things difficult because there would be nothing to grip.

Twenty feet to the undercarriage, however, would only demand six feet more to gain the top of the machine, if he could possibly make it. So he waited, crouched in readiness. When the next one came—and he prayed that it would be one which was heading for the planet's exterior and not to the city—he flew upwards from his crouching position, his hands outflung. But his timing was bad. The machine had passed when he reached the point where it had been, nor had he been quite high enough.

Gently he floated down again, settled himself, and waited once more. This time there was a long interval before anything happened, but presently he detected the twin lights in the distance which denoted a 'plane's approach. He began to prepare, counting the seconds to himself so as to be sure of his timing . . . .

He leapt, hurtling upwards with hands clawing desperately at the air. It was quite the mightiest leap of his life. It carried him to the level of the plane's summit and his hands caught tightly hold of projections on the bodywork. Panting hard he hung on for a moment and then began to drag himself upward.

Everything depended now on whether the machine was making for the city or the exterior. Lying flat on his face and hanging on he watched developments—and for a moment or two thought the city was the pilot's destination. Then the course changed suddenly and the machine's nose tilted to such an angle that Clay thought he was going to be thrown off. He clamped his knees against the smooth bodywork and gripped the metal projections until he felt that his fingers would break.

So, finally, at a nearly vertical angle, the queer wingless machine darted into an enormous shaft in the cavern roof and began sweeping upwards at dizzying speed. Clay could feel wind rushing past him and he was nearly upright in position, so steep was the flyer's angle. Around him the shaft was dark, except 'for the glow cast by the plane's own lights.

It seemed to him that the ascent lasted an interminable time and he wondered vaguely how long he would be able to hold on—then abruptly the darkness had gone and the machine was soaring swiftly into the Martian noonday sky. Slowly the vessel flattened out and Clay was able to look about him.

It was his first glimpse of Mars' surface at close quarters, and as far as he could see it looked like the Sahara back home, except that the sand was reddish instead of pure yellow. Everywhere the sand extended, sometimes in flat plains; at others rising into towering dunes. The air was thin and cool, so thin indeed that Clay found it hard to breathe after the pressurised underworld. There were no clouds in the pale blue sky. A sun, much smaller than that seen from Earth, was about at the zenith-line. Yes, it was around noon.

Clay moved a little and made himself as comfortable as possible. What happened next he did not know. He had to remain where he was until the machine landed, unless he wanted to risk a two-hundred-foot jump to the desert. He felt that he was reasonably safe since the pilot would not be able to see him lying flat on the plane's summit.

And the machine travelled on and on, across endless wastes, broken here and there by a green line which extended from horizon to horizon, part of the underworld shaft-system but looking—from the standpoint of Earth at least—like a canal. Clay looked down on the rank, queer vegetation flourishing in the metal line and decided it must be of the same order as verdigris, except that was a vegetational outcropping and not a deposit of acetate of copper.

At last a smudge loomed on the not far distant horizon. Clay watched it intently, and by degrees it took on the form of a city. It was not by any means an architectural masterpiece. Made of solid blocks of stone it had a rough-hewn appearance, the buildings all being one-story and scattered around without any organised plan. In fact the whole semblance of order lay in the streets which radiated from a central one connecting with the desert sands. Lying in the Martian sunlight the town looked like an abandoned relic of a lost race—but not as the 'plane came nearer. Clay could distinctly see Martian men and women in the streets. There were vehicles of sorts—by no means of the design of those in the underworld—and here and there aircraft circled, machines which had obviously been stolen from below.

The flyer began to descend. Clay waited tensely for a chance to drop away without injuring himself. Low over the roofs the 'plane swept, then at last began to level down towards a flat park-like space, its surface covered with sun-hardened clayish soil. It did not improve matters for Clay when he observed a group of Martians, possibly an "airport" crew, waiting for the machine to come in.

He loosened one of his guns from his belt and held it in readiness, then as the machine dropped to within twenty feet of the ground he took a chance and slid free. Normally, he would have landed with considerable heaviness, but the lighter gravity enabled him to fall on his feet, and still keep balanced when he had dropped.

Immediately the groundsmen saw him, and shouted—

but at that moment they had the incoming plane to watch and control, evidently to be assured it did not over-travel its distance on a now projecting landing-gear. Clay swung round and began to run as hard as he could, back towards the desert not very far away which the 'plane had only just crossed.

In enormous leaps and bounds he outdistanced the solitary man who had decided to pursue him—and finally he took a flying leap over a sand-dune and landed in the warm grains on the other side. Here he paused for a while, getting his breath back and looking about him. He knew only too well that his safety was only temporary; before very long the Martians would come after him. He might be able to deal with some of them, but certainly not all. So, what next ?

He wondered whether this particular town was Malacon, the place he wanted. And, if so, whereabouts the Princess Thalia was being kept in captivity. Then as he peered over the dune and studied the town carefully he began to doubt. No principal town could surely be such a hotch-potch of stone buildings ? It was more like a desert outpost. Somehow he had got to find out exactly where he was—which was not going to be easy. It was unlikely that the Martians, granting he could grab one and make him talk, would be able to understand English; and they would certainly make every effort to capture him the moment he showed his face.

In fact matters were much more concrete than this. The Martians were coming after him. He saw them for a moment as he peered over the top of the dune. A dozen strong, coming out of the town's main street and then hurrying across the sand and looking about them. To their rear came a tractor-like affair with four men in it, each of them armed. Clay promptly withdrew his head from the top of the dune and thought swiftly. In a matter of minutes he would be discovered—unless . . . . .

It was the tractor which interested him. Though by no means a fast vehicle it was certainly quicker than any Martian, and probably the only faster conveyance was an air-

plane. If he could somehow work his way round to the rear
of the tractor . . . . In the circumstances it was the only thing
he could do, and even as he thought about it he began
moving, the sand absorbing all sound.

Quickly he hurried round the base of the tall dune,
and followed it to its extremity. He could hear the chugging
engine of the tractor quite distinctly now. Risking discovery
he climbed the sloping sandbank and peered over the top.
Just as he had hoped, the Martians were now in front, and
he behind them. The tractor was about six yards away and
moving on.

Clay did not hestitate a moment longer. He whipped
out his second gun and leapt across the intervening distance,
firing as he went. Because the guns made no sound he had
the advantage and three of the men in the tractor dropped
before they knew what had hit them. The fourth kept his
hands on the controls, watching Clay fixedly as he gained
the vehicle and scrambled into it over the bodies of the
fallen men.

"Keep driving," he said briefly, and whether the Martian understood or not he did not know. In any case the
giant kept operating the steering gear, his malevolent eyes
glancing from the desert back to Clay.

The Martians who were walking ahead were too intent
on their job to glance back. They could undoubtedly hear
the tractor on the move which to them was enough guarantee
that all was well. Just why the tractor was being used at
all Clay had no idea—until he caught sight of boxes of
ammunition stowed into a cupboard-like affair near the con-
trol-board. Then he understood. Evidently the thing was
a travelling arsenal in case finding him was going to prove
dangerous.

"Is this town Malacon?" Clay demanded, of the Martian, and he looked puzzled.

"Malacon?" Clay insisted, and pointed back with his
left hand gun to the town.

At this the Martian seemed to understand. He said

something unintelligible and shook his head at the same time
—which was enough for Clay. He moved his gun significantly, ordering the Martian out of the tractor.

The giant creature hesitated, until both guns jabbed
him fiercely—then he turned from the controls and, helped
by a shove from Clay, he half fell out of the tractor into the
sand. From this second onwards Clay knew the whole thing
was up to him.

He did not know how to control the tractor, but it was
still chugging along steadily. He went on his knees, so
his head was not visible, and gripped the steering wheel.
A quick survey of the levers suggested that the mechanism
was simplicity itself. He pushed what he took to be the
accelerator and the tractor immediately gathered speed.

By this time the Martian who had been pitched into the
sand was yelling to his comrades. They swung round, just
in time to see the tractor—Clay having no idea where he was
driving—bearing down upon them. Desperately they hurled
themselves out of the way, cursing in their own language
as a deluge of sand swept over them amidst exhaust fumes.

Clay put on speed. He could hear the yells but did
not risk raising his head to look. It was just as well he
didn't for the back of the tractor glowed for a moment where
a beam hit it. Metal turned milky white under heat and
then hardened again into a wrinkled oval.

Against the rising speed of the tractor, sand flying
around it in a fountain, the Martians stood no chance. They
ran for a little way, firing savagely with their ray-pistols,
but Clay was soon out of range. When the shouting had
died down with distance he ventured to peer over the tractor's edge and saw the Martians were quite half a mile away,
staring after him. He grinned to himself, then released the
steering wheel for a while and busied himself with heaving
overboard the bodies of the three Martians he had wiped
out. This done he felt free to decide on his next move.

If there was one. He had no means of knowing where
he was heading. That the town he was fast leaving behind

was not Malacon was the only fact he had gained. Malacon itself might be just anywhere in the wilderness. Having no supplies with him, and no water, he might go on travelling endlessly in the Martian wastes, to lose himself and die of thirst. Or . . . as was more likely . . . an airplane would be sent out to locate him, probably kill him. Since this seemed a likely possibility he moved the ammunition boxes out of their cupboard-like recess. It left just enough room for him to squeeze in and have a metal protection over his head if the worst came to pass.

These preliminaries attended to there was no alternative but to keep on driving and trust to luck. During the day-light hours there was considerable danger of recapture, but by night he might be able to do many things. Night, how-ever, was some six hours away, since Mars spins at approx-imately the same revolution speed as Earth. Then there was the matter of fuel. How long could the tractor hold out ?

Finally Clay ceased worrying and kept on driving, hoping he would sight something interesting before long. He put on all the speed the tractor could take and continued a forty-mile-an-hour advance.

It was the very smallest thing which gave him a clue. He chanced to be looking into the distances away from the sun when he caught sight of a solitary speck dropping from the cloudless heaven, to vanish over the horizon. It had been a 'plane without doubt, and it had landed somewhere. Possibly a town. So Clay swung the tractor round and headed in the direction the speck had taken.

He had covered perhaps half the distance over the wilderness when a glance back made him start. Far away as yet, but coming nearer, was a fleet of aircraft, low down over the desert. He needed no imagination to realise they must be searching for him. Promptly he stopped the tractor, put his guns more comfortably in his belt, then jumped over into the sand. He ran for a considerable distance towards a hum-mock of sand and then dropped flat behind it, scooping the grains out quickly with his hands. In the space of perhaps five minutes he had made a hollow deep enough to lie in. Settling into it he dragged the sand in on top of him. Closing his eyes tightly and setting his lips he wriggled himself down until his head too was covered with the grains, there being only just enough clearance for him to suck air through his nostrils.

It was his only possible chance. At close quarters he would be discovered, but from above he would never be seen—nor would a casual glance reveal him as anything more than a rising mound of sand beside the dune, So he waited, perspiring and half choked, for whatever might happen next.

After a long interval he became aware of feet thudding in the sand not far away. Evidently one, or all, of the 'planes had descended to the dessert surface to investigate, which was no more than he had expected. There was nothing he could do but remain motionless and trust that he would not be observed.

The sound of the feet came nearer, then stopped. Clay sweated and sucked in what air he could. It dawned on him that now it was too late that he would have been more sensible to keep one of his guns projected in such a position that he could fire it. . . . Then, unexpectedly, something must suddenly have taken the attention of the searching Martians. There came shouts, obviously of alarm, followed by the running of several pairs of feet—receding gradually. After this all became silent except for a queer moaning noise which Clay was at a loss to understand.

Half stifled as he was he had to take the risk of coming up for air. He dragged his head and shoulders out of the sand, rubbing the grains out of his hair and doing his best to clear his ears. As he did so he looked about him. The Martians had vanished, but their footmarks showed how close they had been. In fact he was certain they must surely have been near enough to observe the trick he had attempted. Why, then, the shouts of alarm and their abrupt departure ?

Puzzled, he got to his feet and gambled his safety far enough to climb to the top of the ridge and see what had happened. He was rewarded by the vision of the deserted tractor and, far away in the sky heading back home, the 'planes which had come out to seek him.

"I don't get it," he muttered, baffled; then he became conscious once again of that strange moaning noise, rising and falling steadily.

He glanced about him—and understood. Far away across the desert a mighty column of darkness was rising from the surface of the wilderness into the sky, slowly blotting out the sun and advancing with incredible speed against Mars' light gravity. The phenomenon was, in fact, a sandstorm-tornado, believed by many Earth students of Mars to exist.

The last thing Clay had ever wanted to do was have experience of one first hand. The very fact that the Martians had flown away quickly to safety was warning enough that hell itself was about to break loose.

Chapter - Four.

THE PRINCESS THALIA.

For several seconds Clay stood watching the whirling sandspout and listening to the steadily increasing roar it gave forth. His survey satisfied him that by no possible method could he hope to avoid it. It was gouging a track through the desert straight to the spot where he was standing, and for quite two miles around it was turning the atmosphere and desert itself into a complete chaos of raging winds and obliterating grains.

He made up his mind quickly. The tractor was possibly heavy enough to escape being blown over and within it were several boxes which had ammunition in them. Clay began moving in prodigous leaps, gained the vehicle, and dragged the boxes out. He tipped the ammunition into the sand and then smashed the boxes in pieces—four sides and a base, against the tractor's chain wheels. The resulting wood planks, small though they were, were just big enough to block the empty space under the tractor's belly. He left enough room to crawl into the little space, then he curled up, thrust the last piece of wood into place, and hoped for the best.

Makeshift though his shelter was, it served its purpose. With a blasting roar the sandstorm-tornado burst about him and for several minutes the area was a screaming, blinding mass of grains and hurricane wind. Sand blew in everywhere, the tractor rocked and swayed, but it did not overbalance—until at last the chaos began to abate and Clay, for the second time, brushed the grains from himself and wriggled out of his hole.

Standing up he saw the storm was on its way across the desert. Behind it the desert was changed. The dune which had afforded him shelter had been levelled. The tractor was completely buried and become a dune in itself—and therein, he realised, lay a great advantage. Inevitably a search would be made for him again, but with the main landmark of the tractor gone, what then ?

The rest of the job was up to him. All pointers as to his position had disappeared. He had to keep on going towards the distant smudge he had seen—in the hope it was Malacon—and hide himself in the grains at the first sign of planes on the search. Soon it would be dark, anyway. The cleared sun was already half way to the horizon.

So he set off, beginning to feel the miseries of thirst, but not particularly fatigued. The sun being further from Mars than the Earth its intensity in these desert wastes was not intolerable, and the lightness of the gravity also helped him to keep up his energy.

It had come to the short Martian twilight, and he had covered five miles with prodigous speed, when a glance over his shoulder showed him search planes in the distance. Instantly he lay down, wriggled himself into the grains, and then lay face up watching the sky.

For half an hour he watched the searchers gliding and sweeping aimlessly like carrion-crows; then with surprising suddenness the night closed down. It was instantaneous and complete, the stars gleaming forth abruptly as though somebody had switched on a host of lights. Thankful for the protection Clay struggled up and continued on his way, refreshed by the cool wind which had already commenced to blow across the great spaces.

A sudden brilliant light casting a shadow of himself ahead—a shadow which changed direction rapidly—made him spin round. He expected to see the beam of a 'plane searchlight upon him, but instead he beheld the busy little moon of Phobos, which being only 5,800 miles from Mars completes a circuit of the primary three times in twenty four hours. Rising from the west, and arcing slowly across the sky towards the east, it made for Clay a fascinating picture— had he been in the mood to appreciate it.

And before he had proceeded very far the much more leisurely second moon—Deimos—appeared, adding its light to that of its companion. Clay kept on going steadily, in leaps and bounds where he could, his shadow duplicated and the light constantly changing as Phobos hurried on his way across the Martian heaven.

By this time thirst was becoming a very real problem to Clay, but he had to endure it because there was no other course. He put mile after mile behind him, pausing ever and again for rest and to survey the weird sky or possibility of airplane pursuit. Apparently, however, the search had been abandoned, unless an unpleasant surprise was in store for him later.

Ultimately, however, the smudge that had been on the horizon was no more than perhaps a mile away, a fact which could be accounted for by the Martian horizon being nearer than Earth's, and also because Clay himself had moved at three times normal walking speed.

Licking his parched lips with an equally dry tongue he surveyed his destination in the twin moonlights. Here and there a light gleamed from a window; in the streets there was a steady glow. The whole impression was of considerable numbers of stone buildings, white in the pallid glimmer, and of streets crossing and intercrossing one another. Here was a town of fair size, with every possibility of being Malacon. Clay began to hurry his pace in the hope that his ordeal in the desert was nearly finished.

As in the case of the other Martian town, this one also extended into the desert, where it came to an abrupt end. Clay soon covered the odd mile between himself and the nearest main street and then watched the comings and goings of Martian men and women amidst the glow of the overhead lights. They moved about as much as Earth people might do in a city, sometimes in couples, sometimes alone. They went in and out of the buildings, or entered vehicles and drove away. The whole business was entirely orderly and normal.

To go up one of these main streets, as Clay realised, was asking for it, so he detoured to the rear of the buildings where the lights were dim. And here disaster overtook him. Before he had the chance to realise what had happened three Martians bore down on him from the shadows and seized him tightly, whipping away his guns.

"Okay, so you win," he said bitterly, too exhausted to struggle any longer. "I might have known it !"

The Martians did not comment. Keeping a firm grip on him they led him back into the main street and into a queerly designed vehicle which was waiting for them—possibly the equivalent of an Earth police car.

Clay sat in morose silence as he was whirled through the city's main streets, until finally an imposing looking building of dark stone was gained. He was led into it, hardly caring what happened next, through a lighted hall, and then into the equivalent of an office. The next thing he fully realised was that he was face to face with Lexas. He was seated at a plain desk, his cruel face grinning in cold satisfaction.

"Welcome back, Earthman," he said dryly, and then nodded to the guards so that they backed to the door and remained there.

Clay looked about him. The room was more suggestive of a cell than an office with its friendless grey stone walls and single barred window. The only furniture appeared to be the desk and chair, both large to accommodate Martian size, and the metal cupboard in the corner which looked as though it might be used for files and records.

"You need a drink, my friend," Lexas commented, and got to his feet. He went to an inlet door in the stone wall, tugged it open, and brought forth some of the familiar yellow wine of Mars. Clay watched it greedily as a thin glass was filled to the brim with the liquid.

"The desert," Lexas continued, returning with the filled glass in his hand, "is a thirsty place. You gave us quite a chase . . . ." He held out the glass, then as Clay made a grab at it the Martian inverted it suddenly and watched the liquid pour away along the stone floor.

"You filthy swine !" Clay shouted hoarsely, his throat cracking. "What good does it do you to cheat me of a drink ? You want my body in good condition, don't you, for·that stinking experiment of yours ?"

"You will survive quite a while yet without liquid," Lexas responded, perching his huge body on the edge of the desk and surveying Clay with his deadly eyes. "I think you should know, Earthman; that I have not enjoyed chasing you all the way from the underground. It has taken up much valuable time . . . but there was nobody else to whom I could entrust the search. You were observed, my friend, by night-lenses from our 'planes as you moved through the moonlight. It was plain that you were heading for Malacon. All we had to do was come on in advance and . . . er . . . welcome you."

"This is Malacon then ?" Clay asked. "That's one thing I was wondering about."

"I do not see that the information can be the least use to you, unless you are under the mistaken impression that I intend to allow you to escape again. Believe me, Earthman, your adventures are over. Now I have captured you I intend to follow out my plan. You will come back with us to the underworld and the Atlantean surgeons will set the robots in action to perform the operation I mentioned . . . . One thing I will grant you," Lexas added.

"What ?" Clay licked his parched lips and gazed longingly towards the bottle of wine in the recess, the door of which was still swinging open.

"You are entitled to be introduced to your partner in the surgical experiment—the Princess Thalia. After your efforts to reach her you deserve that reward."

Clay shrugged as Lexas motioned the guards. Interested though he was in seeing the girl he had struggled—unavailingly—to help, Clay's main desire at the moment was to slake his raging thirst. He fingered his throat and swallowed hard; then unable to contain himself any longer he hurtled suddenly across the room and grabbed the wine container, tipping the cold liquid into his mouth. He gulped and swallowed and breathed hard, expecting any moment that the container would be snatched from him. Instead, when for the moment he was satisfied and put the container back in the recess, he found Lexas smiling at him coldly.

"Perhaps just as well," he said, shrugging. "As you remarked, your body must be in good shape for analysis . . ."

He paused and turned as the door opened before the guards. Between their gigantic figures a slender girl in a sleeveless and backless purple gown was standing. Clay forgot everything for a moment as he studied her.

She was perhaps five feet seven, regal in her carriage despite the fact that she was a prisoner. Grace and symmetry was in every line of her figure. Her shoulder length hair was deep yellow, her face oval with rather high cheekbones and a firm, full-lipped mouth. Her eyes, a deep sea-green, looked at Clay steadily and he saw her lips part for a moment as she gave a little start of amazement.

"You are looking at Clay Drew, Highness," Lexas said, with a gesture. "He has been fool enough to chase all the way from your underworld city in the hope that he might find you—maybe even rescue you."

"A man who will do that is not a fool. He has commendable courage," the girl answered quietly, and her eyes were still fixed on Clay's grim, greasy features.

"Well, here is your Princess," Lexas said, glancing at Clay. "A pity the circumstances are not more congenial for you."

"Am I allowed to speak ?" Clay asked curtly, and the Martian gave a shrug.

"I cannot see that it matters. I would merely warn you that any disrespectful comment concerning myself or my rule will not be tolerated."

Clay moved forward until he was a foot away from the girl. He could tell from the expression on her delicate-featured face that she was his immediate friend—and a grateful one.

"I have to come before you with an apology, Highness," he said. "Ever since I vowed to Kladnor that I would accept the responsibility of being Emperor I have done all in my power to reach you—and if possible effect your rescue. Unfortunately I have failed. Lexas has his own plans—of which you may perhaps know?"

"I know," the girl assented quietly. "You would have made a magnificent Emperor, Earthman."

"For the little time we have why not call me Clay? I like it better that way."

"If you wish it, Clay—though I find the name strange."

"I regret, Highness, that you will not have time to accustom yourself to it," Lexas remarked. "We must commence the return to the underworld immediately. I would offer you both refreshment but, as you may know, an operation is easier to perform when the patients have been without food for some considerable time."

"That mean these pigs have been starving you?" Clay asked the girl abruptly.

"Yes." She shrugged her graceful shoulders. "And not only that. They have been most anxious to persuade me to reveal some of the deeper secrets of my city. That I have declined to do."

"Secrets which you alone know, Highness, otherwise one less important than yourself might have been tempted to speak," Lexas said. "Later, perhaps, you will think better of your stubbornness. The analytical study of a body is not at all pleasant, it being impossible to give anaesthetic and study physical reactions simultaneously."

Clay gave a murderous look and clenched his fists, but

at the moment there was nothing he could do. Lexas had his gun in his hand, and the two guards were also ready for immediate action.

"Bring them out to the plane," Lexas ordered, getting up from the desk edge and striding towards the door. "We have wasted time enough here. It was no use bringing Her Highness to the underworld until we were sure of the Earthman . . . ."

He disappeared through the doorway and Thalia was swung about roughly by one of the guards, the other one remaining to keep an eye on Clay. Clay gave a grim look and then followed the girl out into the corridor. In a moment or two he had caught up with her, Lexas striding on ahead.

"Courage," Clay murmured, giving the girl's slender fingers a squeeze. "Maybe we haven't pulled every trick yet."

"Maybe you have not," she answered, a little droop at the corners of her mouth. "For myself I've exhausted all ideas as far as escape is concerned."

Neither of them said any more. Hard jabs from the guns of the guards made them realise that conversation was not permitted, so thereafter they sank into their own thoughts. When the 'plane was reached they were separated from each other by being forced to take seats at the opposite sides of the cabin. Since Lexas and one of the guards kept a constant eye on them there was just nothing they could do ; so the journey back across the desert began, the remaining guard at the controls.

In perhaps thirty minutes the journey was over. The 'plane sped down the underground shaft and landed in a broad parklike space in the centre of the Atlantean city. To Clay's surprise, as he stepped out of the cabin, he discovered that the sunlight had been restored.

"I never thought they'd do it," he muttered, half to himself, with a glance upwards at the brilliant ball of atomic energy.

"Do what ?" Thalia questioned, standing beside him.

"Restore this artificial sun. I wrecked it, and I was hoping the technicians would hold out against restoring it. Evidently I guessed wrong."

"Definitely so," Lexas commented, coming up in the rear. "The Atlantean technicians have as much dislike for physical discomfort and pain as anybody else; they finally agreed to restore the luminary, using a temporary tower and power-house."

"Do you always have to gain your end by violence?" Thalia asked him bitterly. "Is that the only course you can conceive?"

"Can you name a better one, Highness? Understand one thing: I do not care to what lengths I go just as long as I learn every secret in this scientific wilderness of yours. Remember that to me, you, and all like you, are aliens, so why should it disturb me to use persuasion when I want information—But come," Lexas broke off, motioning sharply. "There is much to be done."

He led the way from the landing field through the brilliant glow and Clay and Thalia started to follow him, the guards close behind them. Their journey ended in the bowels of one of the city buildings. Here, in a gigantic room lighted by the usual shadowless globes, there were scientific and surgical instruments of immense complexity, together with operating tables, specially designed chairs, and numberless projectors which probably handled all types of radiation from X-rays.

The door closed. The two guards stood with their backs to it, guns ready. Clay gave a troubled glance around him and then towards the girl at his side. Her profile was towards him, and though her rounded chin was firmly set he fancied he could see it trembling slightly as she tried to master her fears. He did not say anything, however, for the simple reason that he could not see any way out of the situation, either.

Moving to the centre of the laboratory Lexas looked about him and then motioned his arm. In response two

Atlantean workers came into view, both of them white-smocked, of apparent middleage, their powerful faces having the same dull, beaten look so noticeable amongst their colleagues.

"Those two men are the finest surgeons in the city," Thalia whispered to Clay.

"To do the kind of job Lexas has in mind they'll need to be," Clay muttered. "What I don't understand is why Lexas gets his way every time. Surely, having superior intelligence, your people—or rather our people—ought to be able to outwit him ?"

"There are not enough of us, Clay. And besides, we have not used physical violence for centuries and therefore hardly understand it. Our people fall under Lexas' sway because he is so utterly ruthless."

"I'm one who hasn't forgotten how to be violent, anyway," Clay said. "I've already given Lexas one under the jaw, and I'll do it again, with interest, before I'm finished. These brutes don't want dealing with by science, Thalia—they want the business end of a gun."

"I hope your talk is not useless," the girl said dispiritedly. "Lexas has gained his end so far, and he looks likely for going on doing it."

She said no more as Lexas turned and came towards her, the two Atlantean surgeons at his side.

"I have outlined the nature of the operation to these two men," he said briefly. "They understand the details fully. You and the Earthman both know what is intended. I require an analysis of your respective physiques so that synthetic beings can be made in the hundreds like you, to carry the brains of myself and my fellows when we travel to Earth. My ambition is to conquer that world and live on its surface. The instruments and valuable scientific equipment that is in this underworld will be transferred to Earth by degrees."

"And be useless," Thalia said. "You don't understand one half of the instruments, and you never will. It would take a creature of your low order of intelligence many centuries to understand even the simplest of our machines. What do you know of solar energy, fourth dimensional conversion, mathematical catalysts, and the like ?"

"You know all about them, Highness," Lexas pointed out. "You have been taught those secrets from the cradle upwards, and as I said earlier I intend to learn everything during the analysis of your body. These surgeons have instructions to protract the most painful parts of their experiment to the limit, and will only desist upon you giving me information I must have. I do not intend to become ruler of machines I do not understand."

"You will find I shall cheat you," Thalia retorted. "I will die before I will speak, and when I am dead my body is no more use to you for analysis than . . . than rock."

"Let me get something straight," Clay said abruptly. "Do you two men"—he looked at the surgeons—"actually mean you are willing to obey this creature's orders to the extent of torturing your Princess, and probably killing her ? In heavens' name what sort of jellyfish are you, anyway. ?"

"We have no alternative," one of them answered. "If we do not obey we shall die."

"Isn't that preferable to betraying your race and killing the girl who is your ruler ? Or was, anyhow."

The men said nothing. They looked at one another and then at Lexas, The Martian giant grinned broadly.

"Proceed with the analysis," he ordered. "If you make any mistakes, aimed at defeating me, you'll be shot dead where you stand. My guards there are within range, remember. Take the girl first : she has information to impart ; the Earthman has not."

At that the surgeons came forward and seized Thalia's arms tightly. She struggled a little but had no chance in their grip. It was too much for Clay. He flung himself forward to assist her, only to go reeling from a smashing blow in the mouth from Lexas. Clay landed flat on his back, salty blood on his tongue, to find the huge Martian glaring down on him.

"Learn sense, Earthman," he suggested, clenching his great fists. "You no longer have the advantage."

Clay remained where he had fallen, watching in helpless fury as Thalia was raised easily and laid full length on the nearest operating table. In a matter of seconds buckled straps were drawn tight about her waist, ankles, and neck, pinning her arms to her sides. She made no attempt to struggle, knowing it was a hopeless proposition.

Lexas turned from studying Clay and went over to the girl. Her green eyes looked back at him steadily—cold, contemptuous.

"As far as synthesis is concerned," he said, "these two surgeons have told me all I need to know—after persuasion. But you hold the greater secrets, Highness. Solar energy, for instance, providing inexhaustible power. The machines which accomplish the miracle are in operation in this city, handled by technicians of your race, but they will not break down under torture to tell me how they control their apparatus. I hope you will not be so obstinate."

"You are wasting your time," Thalia replied deliberately. "You tried to make me talk when I was in Malacon, with no result."

"Those were mere inconveniences compared to what is to happen now," Lexas said.

To this conversation Clay was not listening very attentively. His attention had strayed from the bound girl on the operating table to the bench quite near to him. Just above it were shelves full of bottles. Though the symbols were strange, being in the Atlantean language, he was scientist enough to recognise some of the elements . . . . One in paticular. The crystals were unmistable to him — grey, frosty-looking, with impure streaks of nitric acid and alcohol running through them.

Clay acted with lightning speed. Utilising the light gravity he vaulted to his feet and shot forward all in one movement, the guards so astonished at his speed they had

no time to pinpoint him with their guns before he had
snatched up the bottle of crystals and held it over his head.

"Wait," one of the surgeons cried hoarsely, as the guards
prepared to fire. "If you shoot him you'll kill the lot of us."

"Don't I know it ?" Clay breathed, his eyes glinting.
"I've got a weapon in my hand here more powerful than
all your guns put together. Fulminate of mercury. If it
drops . . . as it will if I am shot . . . this laboratory, and
probably the whole building, will be blown to atoms."

Lexas gave the surgeons a grim look. His own knowledge of chemicals was limited, but he could read from the
expressions on the two mens' faces that they were genuinely
afraid.

"Release that girl " Clay ordered, coming forward with
the jar in his hand.

No moves were made—so he tossed the jar in the air
and then caught it again. He felt sweat break out on his face
at the chance he had taken. Lexas stood undecided, not
sure whether or not a trick was being pulled. To find out the
truth might prove too dangerous for comfort.

"Release her," he said briefly, glancing at the surgeons.
"This fool has only a temporary advantage ?"

"You think so ?" Clay gave a hard grin. "Just start
weighing things up for yourself, Lexas. Nobody dare shoot
me or touch me as long as I hold this jar ! In case you
think I'm pulling a bluff, here's a sample."

Watched in deadly silence, including Thalia who had
fixed her eyes in fascination on the jar, Clay removed the
stopper and very gently extracted a few of the soda-like
crystals. He put the stopper back—then he flung the crystals
with all his power at the opposite metal wall of the surgery.
There was a blinding detonating flash, a report vicious enough
to sting the ear-drums, and dispersing smoke.

"Satisfied ?" Clay asked, thankful his guess about the
stuff had been right. "If that's what two or three crystals
can do you know what this jar full can deal with."

"Step outside this surgery and you'll be shot down,"

Lexas said venomously. "I have given orders to that effect. Now it appears you will be blown to pieces too, along with the men who shoot you. That will not affect me in here, so leave if you wish. I will forego the pleasure of analysis of your living body and use an Atlantean . . . ."

"I'm not going anywhere," Clay interrupted, moving forward.

Lexas said nothing. The two surgeons glanced in surprise at one another. Thalia still watched the jar with hypnotic interest.

"Then what do you intend ?" Lexas demanded.

"It has occurred to me," Clay responded, with a glance about him, "that I am in exactly the right place to get some action. I know by now that escaping from you is no use—and in any case it would not serve a useful purpose any more since Thalia, whom I was seeking, is here beside me. So I have a different plan. Putting it briefly, Lexas, I intend to become you."

The Martian stared in wonder.

"Your own vile experiment gave me the idea," Clay explained. "If, as seems possible, brains can be transferred from a natural body into a synthetic one, and function perfectly, there is no reason why my brain should not be put into your body. Can you imagine what would happen with everybody believing me to be you ?"

"You can't do it !" Lexas shouted, striding forward angrily, only to stop again as Clay raised the jar significantly. "It . . . .it would never work out. It . . . ."

"You mean you hope it won't ! You don't like the idea of your brain being removed, to be put away somewhere in a preserving fluid until—if ever—needed again. The risk is just as bad for me, but I'm prepared to take it, and I'm going to."

"Clay, I don't agree with it," Thalia said urgently. "It may bring about your death—then what shall I do, alone ?"

"If things remain as they are you'll die anyway," Clay reminded her. "And unpleasantly, if Lexas has his way. The

fact remains that only Lexas has any power in this underworld—so if I am to turn the tables on him I must become
him and work things out from there on . . ." Clay looked at
the surgeons. "It can be done ?" he questioned.

"It can," one of them agreed. "And you have great
courage, Earthman."

"There's no question of courage about it; it's simply
necessity. Deep down I'm scared stiff !"

Clay looked across at the two guards by the door and
motioned them: They came forward slowly, their hands on
their weapons, but afraid to use them.

"I'll take those," Clay said, and did so without resistance. He handed them over to Thalia and she took them
gingerly, then to her he added, "While the operation is being
performed, Thalia, I shan't be able to keep things in hand,
of course—so it will be your job. Here—take this jar."

. She did so, her face troubled. "Clay, are you sure that
you are doing the right thing ?" she insisted. "If there is
one small mistake it means . . . ."

"I know only too well what it means, Thalia, and I'm
going through with it."

The girl took the jar and held it well away from her, her
green eyes upon it in horror. Then she moved away from
the operation table as Clay motioned her. He looked at the
grim-faced Lexas and the two guards.

"Her Highness is sufficient guarantee of my safety—and
hers," he said. "You know what it will mean if you dare
attack her . . . . Are you two surgeons ready ?"

The men nodded. Lexas drew away sharply as they
strode towards him. They hesitated, glancing at Clay.

"You think you can do this to me ?" Lexas demanded in
fury. "First you have to get me on the operating table, and
I think I am strong enough to prevent that !"

Clay was silent for a moment, the Martian glaring at him
only a couple of feet away—then Clay acted with the devas-
tating suddenness characteristic of him. He slammed out his
right fist with all his strength, straight into the giant's

stomach. He gulped, his breath exploding in a gasp. His action of doubling forward at the sudden anguish brought his chin within aiming distance, and it felt to him as though a battering ram hit it. Under the impact of the left uppercut he staggered. Another blow before he could regain his balance slewed him half over the operating table. Immediately the surgeons drew tight the strap which held him about the waist. After that the job was easy. Though he threshed and kicked violently he finished up firmly secured, arms pinned to his sides.

"Good enough," Clay said in satisfaction. "Now what happens?"

One of the surgeons walked over to another table and wheeled it forward until it was alongside the one containing the fuming, helpless Martian.

"If you will prepare yourself, Excellency?" the surgeon murmured, looking at Clay.

Clay nodded and lay down full length, making no comment as the straps were drawn about him. Then he smiled as Thalia came to his side, still holding the deadly jar.

"When I asked Kladnor for an Emperor I never thought such a man as you would come," she said. "For my sake, the sake of the race, you are risking death—or perhaps madness."

"As much my race as yours, sweetheart," Clay responded, with a faint grin. "Or did you overlook that I'm descended from Hertis of Atlantis?"

"Such a man as you has never existed in my race for generations," Thalia responded, her green eyes upon him in womanly adulation. "All of us, male and female alike, have become soft through too much comfort. You are of different stock —of the fighters who brought our race to greatness."

Clay did not say anything. The next thing he knew was that she had kissed him and for a moment she stood smiling encouragement down upon him, the jar in her dainty hand and the two guns in the sash about her waist.

Then the anaesthetic cone closed over Clay's face and blotted out the world. His senses started to reel away into a great and soundless darkness.

CHAPTER FIVE.

THE OPERATION.

Clay returned to consciousness to the sound of clinking instruments and the glow of overhead lamps which cast no shadow. He moved stiffly, unaccustomedly, since he was completely unused to the body his brain was occupying. With the help of one of the surgeons he sat up. The man—and his colleague—were both looking anxious.

"Your Excellency feels little the worse?" asked the man supporting Clay.

"Just whoozy," he answered. "I sort of expected I'd be laid out for weeks whilst I recovered from the effects."

"Our surgery is instantaneous," the specialist answered. "Special restoratives make good all the loss of the operation. There is no reason why you cannot walk out of here in almost perfect health."

"Almost," Clay repeated, in a vocal organs so deep he did not recognise them.

"Assimilation takes times," the surgeon explained. "You now have the body of Lexas: it will be some little while before we—and you—are able to judge the results. We have connected the various ganglia of your brain to Lexas' nervous system. It is too early to predict the result."

"I'm not doing this just out of fun," Clay said. "I only

want this body long enough to finish the job I have in mind—then I'm going back to my own flesh and blood. Incidentally, what became of 'me' ?" he asked, looking about him.

"Your body, without the brain, has been safely put away in suspended animation," the surgeon answered. "In a tube approximating absolute zero, at which no molecular activity —and consequently decay—can exist."

"And Lexas' brain ?"

The surgeon nodded towards a huge sealed globe nearby. Clay gave a little shudder at the vision of the perfect brain floating in deep blue preservative.

"I don't suppose he likes the situation a bit," he commented; then as the straps were unbuckled from him he slid from the operating table and tested his enormous limbs and body. They felt heavy, because they were natural to the gravity of the planet, but otherwise he was in no way incommoded.

Moving experimentally he looked across to where Thalia was seated. She looked tired and anxious, jar in one hand and guns in the other. Near to her, their faces grim, were the two guards who had not dared in the interval to make a move. They looked at Clay fixedly as he approached, obviously trying to fathom whether he was really Clay or their leader.

When he got close to the girl and met the look in her green eyes Clay hesitated. He was conscious for the first time of something wrong. It took him a moment or two to realise what it was: then he knew. She no longer had any attraction for him !

"It's ridiculous !" he whispered, half to himself, puzzled.

"Clay, is it you ?" Thalia rose to her feet and stood gazing up into his eight feet of height. "Though I watched the operation performed I can't believe it somehow."

"Yes—it's me—Clay. At least I think so . . . "

Clay stopped again, frowning with muscles which felt taut and uncomfortable. This girl, who before the operation had seemed so wholly desirable, so completely in line with everything he had ever pictured in a woman, was now indescribably revolting. Her face, her figure, her entire manner, infuriated him. So much that when she put a gentle hand on his arm he shook it away impatiently.

"Leave me alone !" he snapped.

She gazed up at him in wonder, then half in fear. He swung his huge body round and glared at the nearby surgeons.

"What have you too fools done to me ?" he demanded in fury.

They looked at each other in surprise, then as Clay stormed towards them they took a nervous step backwards.

"Something's wrong !" he shouted. "I've more of Lexas in me than Clay Drew ! Her Highness doesn't mean a thing to me anymore. I—I simply loathe the sight of her. And you ! I hate all things that don't look like myself !"

"That, Excellency, is purely a—a ramification of the operation," the chief surgeon explained hastily. "It will pass off. Since you are using Lexas' body you are impregnated with certain of his characteristics . . . ."

"Why the devil should I be ?" Clay interrupted harshly.

"It is a matter of bloodstream," the surgeon continued. "It feeds the brain, as you know. It is the bloodstream of Lexas and evidently it reacts strangely on a brain accustomed to a different type of blood, just as a machine running on a certain oil will clog when a different oil is used. As for the revulsion you experience at the vision of all beings unlike yourself—that too is part of the inherent Lexas, which we cannot eliminate. He is a pure Martian, remember—or was —and you, and her Highness, and us, are basically of another world. It is the mechanism of heredity, the most complex reaction of all, which is at work on you."

"So that's it." Clay cooled a little. "But you believe it will pass off ?"

"As your brain settles down, yes."

Clay clenched his enormous fists. "I don't like this a bit," he declared. "And the moment I have my plans finished I want my own body back, and feel like a human being again . . . ."

He strode back to where Thalia was standing and took from her the jar and the guns. The jar he returned to the shelf; the guns he put in the belt at his waist, alongside the gun already there.

"Clay," Thalia said quietly. "However you may feel towards me I've got to work beside you. You know that."

"I suppose so," he admitted, scowling. "I would much rather you kept out of my sight. I have the feeling that I may forget myself and deal with you as Lexas might. Don't you understand ? It's something beyond my control !"

"I'll take the risk," she responded. "To me, in spite of your outer appearance and mental turmoil you are still Clay, fighting for our race and enduring the miseries of the damned to do it . . . . You have plans. What are they ?" And the sudden imperiousness in her tone revealed for a moment the generation of rulers from which she had sprung.

"We'll go to Lexas' headquarters and work it out," Clay responded. "This is no place to talk. As for you two men . . . ." Clay looked at the guards and thought for a moment, then he glanced towards the surgeons. "Any way you can put these two men out of commission ?" he demanded, and they looked at each other in alarm.

"Suspended animation, Excellency, if you wish," the chief surgeon responded. "In that way they can do no harm and will only revive whenever you wish it."

Clay nodded ; then as the two guards realised what was in store for them they tried to escape—until Clay's vast hands seized the back of their necks and whirled them round. Huge though they were they lacked six inches of his own enormous height.

"No you don't my friends," he said grimly. "You don't suppose I intend to allow you to leave here and reveal

to your comrades that I am Clay Drew in the body of Lexas,
do you ?"

He whirled them away fiercely, so that they stumbled
towards the surgeons.   The surgeons were ready for the
moves.   Taking a guard apiece they stabbed quickly with
hypodermic needles — and evidently there was something
pretty potent in the syringes for in a matter of seconds each
man sagged to the floor and became motionless.

"You can leave the rest to us, Excellency," the chief
surgeon said.   "They will not awaken until you give the
word.   All we have to do is transport them to the suspended
animation tube."

Clay looked at the motionless bodies, then up to the
big globe wherein there floated the brain of Lexas

"Is that brain alive ?" he asked, pondering.

"Very much so," the surgeon answered.   "But dissocia-
ted from the body it can do nothing.   It can receive impressions and give them forth mentally, but cannot translate them
into physical action.   In fact Lexas must be undergoing the
limit of fine torture. Helpless, fully alive, yet cut off from the
living."

"Would it not be better to destroy that brain ?" Thalia
asked.   "What point is there in keeping it alive ?   It only
belongs to the greatest enemy of the Atlantean race."

"Death is too easy for it," Clay replied, his ugly mouth
setting.   "A little lingering misery won't do Lexas any harm.
In fact he's earned it—not so much for what he had done
as for what he intended to do."

"To me ?" Thalia asked quietly.   "I can forgive that
—now."

"I was thinking of his plans against the Earth, Thalia,
as well as against you . . . ."   Clay shook his head.   "No, let
him live on—eternally if need be.   Now, Thalia, come with
me."

The girl nodded and accompanied him from the laboratory.   His ruthlessness of outlook she put down entirely to

the effect of Lexas' bloodstream, which in truth was the main reason. But with Clay there were even more effects than this. Since he was using his own brain he had his own individuality, and inwardly he was appalled at the deadly thoughts which kept on stealing to him. With every passing minute he realised how he was becoming much more of Lexas than himself.

Since he strode beside the girl in leaving the surgical laboratory the Martian guards assumed that she was his captive. They saluted respectfully as he passed; and within ten minutes they had traversed the main street of the city and entered the building which Lexas used as his headquarters. Only when the big private office had been gained, and the door was shut and guards dismissed, did Clay speak.

"Thalia," he said, speaking with obvious effort, "what I have to do I must do quickly. Those surgeons are wrong. I am not outgrowing the bodily influence of Lexas; I am becoming more submerged by it with every second. But if you will stand by me and ignore some of the things I may say to you, I may get through. You . . . understand?"

"Everything, Clay," the girl answered, smiling. "And I shall never cease to be grateful for what you are doing."

"We need food and rest," Clay said abruptly, turning from her. "Over the meal I'll tell you of the plan I have; then when we have rested we can make the first moves towards putting it into effect. Or rather I can. What you have to remember is that you're my prisoner."

He put out his hand to the desk control panel to summon a servant and then paused. The girl looked at him questioningly.

"Something I forgot," he said. "I don't know the Martian language. I can't give orders in English; they'd start to think things."

"There is a way in which you can be taught the Martian language, so that you can speak it fluently, within the space of half an hour," Thalia said. "It is one of the many scientific accomplishments my race—our race—possesses. It is done by a mental recorder. Just as the ear can listen to a record or sound tape and learn—so in this case the brain absorbs the impressions from the instrument, which on this occasion will be concerned with the Martian language, and the information gained thereby never fades and is indelibly impressed."

"That would solve the problem," Clay admitted. "Where is this instrument? In the laboratories, I suppose?"

"Yes." Thalia considered the matter for a moment and then said, "We could go to the laboratory in question. It would look as though I am still your captive and that I have agreed to show you how that particular machine works. Nobody will interfere with you since you are the ruler, and where men or women of our own race speak to you you can answer in English. If you care to come now I can show you everything."

Clay wasted no further time. He headed for the door, opened it, and the girl stepped out ahead of him into the corridor, taking care to make her manner seem suitably dejected. Not that it was much effort since she was nearly asleep as she walked about after the experiences through which she had passed . . . .

One of the many fast-moving conveyances, a Martian driver at the controls, whirled them to the chief laboratory within five minutes, and once within the wilderness the girl went straight across to the "Impressor," as she called it, with Clay behind her. The fact that he was there—the all-powerful Lexas—was sufficient to deter any movement on the part of the laboratory staff, all Atlantean men and women working under the heavy guard of Martians.

To Clay, the experience of having an entire language impressed on his brain at one sitting was miraculous in the extreme. Thalia put two electrodes to the top of his skull—whilst he sat in a soft leather seat beside the instrument—and then she threw a switch. Needles quivered on their dials under the movement of her hands upon knobs and graded pointers. To Clay, the recipient of the information the machine was giving forth, the effect was as though he were receiving a long series of inspirations concerning a language, each inspiration being so vivid he could not forget it. Until finally, when the machine was shut off, he realised in astonishment that every detail of the Martian tongue was perfectly clear.

"In order ?" Thalia murmured, and he gave a nod.

"Come with me !" he commanded in Martian, getting to his feet. "For you to have broken down far enough to show me how this Impressor works is sufficient guarantee that you can be made to talk of other machines."

The Martian guards in the distance heard the words distinctly and grinned in satisfaction at their "leader's" victory over Thalia's stubbornness. With her head hanging listlessly and Clay following behind her she left the laboratory. In the corridor he caught her arm, so tightly that he felt her wince.

"Sorry," he said roughly, seeing the pained surprise in her green eyes as she looked up at him. "I'm having a ghastly fight to keep myself from hurting you, Thalia. I'm waging two wars at once—one against Lexas and the other against myself. Somehow I've got to keep enough of Clay in my mind to get this job done. All the time I'm with you I want to do just as Lexas wanted to do—to break you down and learn all the scientific secrets of the race. I cannot convince myself that you will tell them all to me of your own free will."

Her only response was to look troubled, half-fearful. She was haunted by the thought that Clay might find the bio-mental struggle too much for him and succumb before he could put into action whatever plan it was he had in mind.

It was when they had returned to the private office—and he had ordered a meal to be sent in—that he began to explain his scheme. He stopped for a while as the servant appeared and set the meal forth, then when he and Thalia were alone again he resumed. "I suppose," he asked, "you have radio equipment powerful enough to reach Earth ?"

"By short wave, yes," Thalia assented. "In fact we have often listened to Earth broadcasts which is how we know the language you speak."

"Of course." Clay put a hand to his forehead worriedly. "Kladnor told me that much; I'd completely forgotten. I'm fogged and bewildered on many things—Anyway, you have radio, which is one good thing. My idea is this: I want from you every detail of your most dangerous scientific equipment —in the way of weapons, I mean—and Earth engineers must duplicate those weapons."

It seemed that Thalia's expression changed a little.

"And then ?" she asked, her voice so low she sounded almost disinterested.

"Then I will tell the Martians that I have decided synthesis is not practicable : that we can go to Earth as we are, in our present physical vestment, and survive. If I, as Lexas, say that, they will have to believe it. So, every Martian embarks for Earth in a series of saucer-machines yet to be constructed ; but once they reach Earth the trap will close ! In fact it will be a double trap. On the one hand the extra gravity of Earth and heavier air will render them physically weak, and on the other the scientific engines of destruction which will be turned on them will destroy them utterly. In that way the whole Martian race can be destroyed. Or at least the part of it which matters. Those left behind can be dealt with by your own scientific weapons."

There was a long silence. Thalia drank some wine and considered, then her frank green eyes looked across the table.

"I don't know how you are going to take this, Clay," she said slowly, "but—I won't do it."

Clay stared at her through the boring eyes of Lexas. She averted her glance, horrified by the rising anger she saw in those baleful orbs. Already fighting a battle to keep his hands off her, this sudden frustration had weakened Clay's defences enormously.

"You won't do it ?" Clay repeated. "Then for why am I scheming and plotting ? The first scheme I suggest—and which is quite workable—you turn down ? Why ?" he snapped angrily. "What's holding you back ? Consideration for this foul race which is overrunning your city and planet ?"

"No, Clay, not that. It's just that I . . . Well, I don't trust Earth men."

"But that's crazy ! I am an Earthman ! You can't have forgotten that."

"You are different to the ordinary run of them : I told you that long ago. Besides, you are a descendant of my own race, which is a very good reason for trusting you. But I know what the rest of Earthmen—and women—are like. Radio reports from Earth have not been encouraging. If I were to part with scientific secrets such as we have here Earth people would be too busy destroying themselves to bother about the Martian invasion."

"I don't believe it," Clay said deliberately. "Attack by a common foe would weld all Earth nations together."

"I'm sorry, Clay. Im not taking that chance."

"You infernal little idiot !" Clap sprang to his feet, overturning the laden table in his fury. Almost before he knew it he had brought his great hand down across the girl's face with savage force. The blow knocked her right out of her chair and she sprawled on the floor, staring up at him with tears in her eyes.

"I—I shouldn't have done that," he whispered, fighting to get himself controlled again. "It wasn't me, Thalia. God knows it wasn't !"

He helped her to her feet. He intended to do it gently, but in spite of his good intentions he was brutally rough about it. He seized her arm and dragged her up, then held on to her and glared down into her face.

"Don't keep crossing my plans, Thalia, or God knows what I may do," he whispered. "The least check to me is like a light to gunpowder."

Thalia dragged her arm free and fingered the smarting flesh tenderly.

"It's not going to work out, Clay," she said, after a long pause. "The body of Lexas is no use to you: it is slowly overpowering you. The only thing to do is change back. I would prefer to lose every battle—even to die—than have Clay Drew, Earthman and would-be emperor, overwhelmed by an alien blood-stream."

"Listen, Thalia, I think we . . . "

Clay broke off and turned as an instrument on the desk buzzed sharply for attention. He turned to it, trying to solve what the instrument was for—then he understood as Thalia raised a single earpiece and handed it to him.

"It's a transmitter-receiver," she explained in a low tone. "Judging from the panel signal the call is from the surgical laboratories."

"Yes ?" Clay asked, in the Martian language. "Lexas speaking."

"You are needed in the surgery, Excellency, came the voice of the head surgeon, and he sounded unaccountably gloomy.

"Why ?" Clay demanded impatiently. "I'm busy."

"I must insist on it, Excellency. It concerns Lexas."

"Lexas ? Oh very well—I'll come."

Puzzled, Clay put the instrument down and looked at the girl. Briefly he recounted the conversation from the other end.

"You'd better go," she said. "If it concerns Lexas it must be important. I'll stay here . . . ."

"No. You'd better come with me. You are still supposed to be my captive."

So, feeling a little more like Clay and less like Lexas for the moment Clay took the tired girl's arm and led her out of the office. When they reached the main surgery and opened the door they received a staggering shock.

A yard or two away, smiling coldly, Clay's figure was standing—just as it had been before the brain operation had taken place.

Chapter Six.

MARS CALLING EARTH.

For Clay himself in particular the shock was overpowering. To see his own body walking and moving towards him, to see the cold smile on the ruggedly chiselled features. In the background the two surgeons hovered.

"What's happened ?" Clay demanded in consternation, holding on to Thalia tightly and watching "himself" approach.

"I can explain it easily enough . . . ."

Clay listened to his own voice in dazed wonder, then cast a glance at Thalia. Her eyes were fixed on Clay's figure intently.

"Yes, it's quite simple, really." Somewhere in the tone of Clay's vocal chords there was the merciless inflexion of Lexas himself. "I am Lexas, in your body, Earthman—just as you are in mine. I hardly think you will call the exchange unreasonable. In fact I would go so far as to say you have improved my own plan immensely."

"Damn your plan !" Clay roared at him, striding forward. "How did your brain ever get out of that jar ?"

"I'll leave it to our medical experts to tell you," Lexas responded, and motioned the surgeons forward. Only the chief advanced, and began talking. A mixture of horror and apprehension was registered on his face.

"We overlooked a vital thing, Excellency," he said. "I

do not think we can be blamed for it because, so far, brain exchange has never been undertaken and . . . ."

"Come to the point !" Clay yelled at him. "How in cosmos did this devil ever get his brain into my body ?"

"It began with hypnosis," the surgeon answered. "As I told you, that brain in the preserving fluid was very much alive, but sundered from a body. The fact of it being an independent unit, being fed by pure essences instead of a bloodstream—which at the best has clogging qualities within it—increased the power of the brain tenfold. It had no physical shackles. My colleague and I were thrown into a hypnotic state as we worked near it, and were given post-hypnotic orders. I remember I was commanded to remove your body from suspended animation and place this brain within it . . . . I did so, ten minutes after receiving the command. Post-hypnosis was used because the brain could not control me during the actual operation. I acted under mental orders already given."

"In fact," Lexas remarked dryly, "you can imagine my brain, when it was in the preserving fluid, as being like a rusty motor which has dropped into a bath of oil. Suddenly there is ease of action—all hindrance gone. Normally I never had hypnotic power : I only developed it whilst temporarily without a body. But now I have one—yours, Earthman !"

Clay clenched his great fists helplessly, unable to imagine anything worse than his sworn enemy possessing his body.

"I like this body," Lexas said. "It is light and comfortable and, from the muscular point of view, easy to control. I have decided to retain it in readiness for when I go to Earth."

Clay strode forward savagely and gripped Lexas by the neck. It was bewildering to Clay to see his own face contorting under the terrific pressure he put on the windpipe. He relaxed his hold because he could not help himself.

"That is better," Lexas said, pulling himself away. "I have another reason for using this body of yours, Earthman. You will never harm it as long as you think there is a slim

hope of you getting it back—which you never will, of course.
That I consider guarantee enough of my immunity from
harm. When I am amongst my own people they will believe
me to be you, of course, and I shall never convince them
otherwise. So I shall look to you for protection."

"But this situation is impossible !" Clay cried, looking
about him helplessly.

"For you perhaps, not for me," Lexas answered. "I
have the advantage of the kind of body I need for the invasion of Earth. Also, whilst my brain was in the preserving
fluid, I was able to understand everything you said—and I
gathered my bloodstream was having a most peculiar effect
on your brain. Giving you, I think, certain of my characteristics ?"

Clay did not answer. He could only stand and look at
"himself" in dull incredulity.

"Possibly," Lexas continued, "those unpleasant effects
will get worse. I understand that the reason for it is that
you have a very small brain in a very big body, by which
the excessively strong bloodstream causes trouble. Whatever
poisonous waste there was in my bloodstream, you are receiving. I, on the other hand, have a much larger brain
in a much smaller body, and because of the lightness I have,
blood pressure is correspondingly lowered. Further, your
blood characteristics are so—shall I say, evil as mine."

"What you really mean," Thalia said slowly, "is that
you have doomed Clay to destruction ? He will gradually
be overpowered by the body he has taken over ?"

"I am hoping so," Lexas responded. "In the meantime
I have things to do—and you, Earthman, are going to do
them."

Clay laughed shortly. "You think I will aid you after
this ?"

"I do, yes." Lexas was silent for a moment; then
abruptly he gripped Thalia's arm and whirled her to him,
holding her tightly. She had neither the strength nor the
build to drag herself away.

"Every time you disobey my instructions, Earthman, Thalia will suffer," Lexas said deliberately. "Your only way to stop it is to kill or injure me—but I don't think you will It would be too much like committing suicide . . . Later, when you have done all I ask, I shall take your place as the Emperor."

Clay shifted his gaze from Thalia. "You'll what ?"

"Why not ? I confess that I formerly regarded her Highness with considerable distaste because she was not of my race. But now that I have become one of hers—and I like the change. Thanks to the residue of your characteristics, Earthman, I find her Highness highly attractive."

Thalia made a frantic effort to pull herself free, but the powerful hand dragged her back, the fingers crushing into her bare arm.

"I think not, Princess," Lexas murmured, eyeing her.

"Did it ever occur to you, Lexas," Clay asked, "that it might not matter to me what you do with Thalia. I have long been fighting a losing battle in trying to love and respect her as I did when I had my own body. It is possible—even before many hours—that any fate overtaking her, torture included if that is your plan—I shall not be at all concerned as to her fate."

"Clay, you can't say that." Thalia cried desperately. "If you abandon me and I am left to—to this body which was once you, what am I to do ? I would be better off dead !"

For a second or so her appeal to his inner individuality cleared the fogs from Clay's mind. He could even think rationally for a moment.

"Suppose I agree to follow out your orders to the letter, Lexas. Will you guarantee to return Thalia to me ? I will take your word on it if you will take mine."

"Unfortunately the issue does not end there," Lexas responded. "Her Highness has still many secrets to give up, and I mean to have them.'

"If you lay a hand on Thalia, Lexas, I'll kill you !" Clay declared. "It may be my own body but I'd prefer to lose it before I'd let Thalia suffer."

"That is how you feel at the moment," Lexas responded. "You are speaking as Clay, the Earthman, at this juncture. In a while you will again be swayed the other way and not care what happens to her. What you are going to do now Earthman, is to give orders for two hundred space machines to be built, identical to those used by the Atlanteans when they searched for you. The 'flying saucers' as they are called. After that I shall have a large number of synthetic men made, to the identical body of this of yours, which is ideally suited to Earth conditions. You, naturally, will give those orders. Following that images will be made of Thalia for the women of my race."

"And when you set off for Earth ?" Clay asked. "I stay here on Mars, I take it ?"

"If I haven't destroyed you by then—yes. I do not want my body back, so it doesn't matter what happens to it."

"But if I stay behind your whole plan is exposed. I—as you—am supposed to be the one who is leading this invasion of Earth."

"You will simply inform the people that you are going to transfer your brain to one of the images—and then you will disappear from sight, in that body of mine which you have. I will take over. It is all so simple."

Clay said nothing. Back of his mind, in this brief spell of mental clarity, he could dimly see a plan forming which might be to his advantage, but it was too early right now to grasp the full consequences.

"Very well," he said briefly, after an interval. "I'll do as you ask."

Lexas looked vaguely surprised at the ready acquiescence.

"Which leaves only Thalia to be dealt with," he said. He turned to her. "I require every secret. Are you sensible enough to reveal things to me ?"

She did not answer. Her mouth set adamantly. Lexas gave a shrug and turned back to Clay.

"We will go to my headquarters, Earthman," he said. "You will apparently be the captor, having the Princess and the Earthman at your mercy . . ." Lexas paused and thought for a moment, then he changed his mind. "No, on second thoughts it would be better if you conducted us both to the prison in the centre of this town. I had it specially built when I took over control. You remember you awakened in it ? It is fitted with many instruments which have made reluctant Atlanteans talk."

Clay did not say anything. He met the dumb, hopeless look which Thalia gave him.

"We are wasting time," Lexas snapped. "Get on the move, Earthman. I will direct you. And remember—you are the captor. Here, take the Princess."

He pushed her away from him and she caught at Clay's arm. He looked down at her, baffled again by his receding interest in her. Finally he motioned to the surgery door and led the way outside, holding Thalia's arm.

"Whatever happens to me," she whispered, "I shall always believe in you, Clay. Even if I die—as I will before I reveal anything to Lexas."

"Much that I shall do from here on has a reason," Clay said, his voice low. "I only hope I can hold out long enough. Whatever I may seem to do to you which is brutal, please forgive. Dimly I can see a way out of this tangle of switched identities."

He said no more as Lexas came within earshot. So, maintaining his pose as the apparent captor, Clay led the way outside and, at Lexas' command, signalled a vehicle. It took them to the newly built prison within a few minutes and, still under Lexas' directions, Clay led the way past files of guards into the lower depths of the place, past cells which contained fractious Atlanteans who had refused to bow the knee to the conqueror, and finally into a big underground basement brightly lighted and equipped with all manner of queer, even Satanic, instruments.

"You will tell them we are your captives and that they

are to make the Princess speak."

For some reason best known to himself Clay did not demur. He looked at the two guards with cold dignity as they stopped in enquiry.

"I have here the Earthman and the Princess Thalia," he said briefly. "Her Highness is still reluctant to give any information concerning the various machines in this city. You will endeavour to—change her mind."

The guards nodded and gripped Thalia tightly, whirling her to them. She gazed up at Clay in horror, her face pale.

"How can you . . ." she began, and at that he strode forward and slapped her fiercely across the face. Under the pretence of seizing her shoulders and shaking them he muttered a few words "Don't give my Identity away, and reveal everything you can. Trust me !"

She moved away dazedly as the guards tugged at her. Utterly bewildered she did not know whether she was trusting Clay—for himself—or the unstable brain which was ruling him. She tried to imagine why she should reveal everything, to the very creature who could bring death and destruction not only on her own planet and people but upon Earth as well. Between the destruction of two worlds, or at least their complete mastery, was a barrier of silence—which only she could break.

Clay, his mighty arms folded, stood watching as the girl's slender body was secured by heavy straps into an upright framework, so tightly that she could not budge hand or foot.

"Tell them not to leave injuries which are obvious," Lexas murmured. "I need her body for a pattern later on."

Clay repeated the order almost word for word and the two guards nodded. They fixed a broad band of elastic metal about the girl's waist and bolted it to a peculiar machine at the back. She remained motionless, watching, her face white.

"What is that devilish contrivance ?" Clay breathed, his eyes glinting.

"A compressor," Lexas murmured. "It will draw tight when the motor is switched on. Tighter and tighter still. I fancy that long before it can do any actual damage to the Princess she will speak."

Clay breathed hard. His own individuality was prompting him to smash down Lexas with his fists and give the order for the villainy to stop—but on the other hand he had his own plan to work out, and there was no way to do it except by using the girl and playing his part.

"Proceed !" he commanded suddenly, and strode forward to watch the operation more closely and to try and convey by signs to the girl that she could save herself only by giving details of the scientific equipment she understood.

Lexas moved across too, the grim expression on his face —since he was supposed to be Clay—completely masking the exultancy he was experiencing.

The motor switched on and Thalia gasped a little as the elastic metal belt drew tight about her waist. With the seconds its merciless pressure increased. Her breathing began to become laboured but no word escaped her.

"Speak, you little fool !" Clay shouted at her. "That way you can gain liberty ! Reveal your secrets and you will be freed . . . ."

Thalia shook her blonde head dully, biting her lower lip. A little groan escaped her as the deadly belt tightened even more. Only by a tremendous effort could she draw breath at all. Clay strode over to her, catching at her thick hair with his hand and forcing her to look at him.

"Believe me," he whispered, "you must speak. You've got to trust me . . . Speak !" he yelled, so Lexas and the guards could hear him.

"Yes . . . ." Thalia whispered, half chocked with the pressure. "I—I will speak. Bring . . . recorder." Then she became motionless, held from falling only by the straps.

Clay signalled quickly and the motor was cut off and the constricting band released. He freed her and raised her in his arms, carrying her to a nearby bench.

"Fetch a recorder," he commanded of the guards. "Whatever it is. Find out in the main laboratory. If you have trouble in doing so use your guns."

Both the guards nodded and huried away. Lexas came over to where Clay was chafing the girl's limp hands.

"You play your part well, Earthman," he commented. "So well indeed I am somewhat suspicious. If you are working out some scheme of your own I would warn you to be careful !"

Clay did not answer. He kept up his efforts to revive the girl and gradually her eyelids opened. She looked at him fixedly.

"You gave your promise, Highness," Lexas remarked. "I am expecting you to keep it."

Thalia hesitated, her eyes on Clay. Then she gave a slow, reluctant nod.

"I gave my word," she responded. "I shall keep it."

There was silence for a moment as she looked into Clay's baleful eyes in puzzled enquiry. He could not answer her unspoken questions because Lexas was too close. All he could do was to grip her hand gently.

Then the two guards returned with the recording equipment, an object rather like a radio set with two spools and a length of recording tape stretching between them. They plugged the apparatus in close to the girl as she still lay half on the bench; then taking the microphone in her hand she began speaking.

Altogether she talked for close on half an hour, and at the end of that time she had described in detail the operation, construction, and capabilities of all the major scientific instruments in the main laboratory, including details of all engines of destruction. The task done she put down the microphone and looked at Clay steadily. He had no expression on his face. In fact his thoughts were dwelling at the moment on the pleasurable realisation that his brain was becoming more and more his own with every passing minute. Evidently the surgeons had spoken truth. Now his new-found physique was settling down to the "left over" effects in Lexas' bloodstream were beginning to count less and less.

"Quite satisfactory, Princess," Clay said after a pause, taking the spooled tape from the equipment. "Now come with me. And you, Earthman."

"You will need that recorder to play the reel back in your headquarters," Lexas reminded him.

Clay motioned one of the guards to bring the instrument along, then he moved to the door and opened it. Some fifteen minutes later he, Thalia, and Lexas were in the big office again, the recorder on the desk, the room cleared of guards.

"Well, you got your wish," Clay said grimly, contemplating Lexas as he lounged in a chair. "What is your next bright idea ?"

"I intend to spend a couple of days studying your recording, Princess," he said, glancing at her as she lay slumped half asleep in a chair nearby. "Thank you for being so explicit. With so many secrets revealed there is little I cannot do."

"For the time being, Thalia, you are a guest," Clay decided. "I shall put a suite of rooms at your disposal."

"Strange behaviour for a captor," Lexas said, with a sharp glance.

"I don't care if it is. Thalia has gone through quite enough, and whilst you study that record she can have some peace."

"As you wish." Lexas gave a shrug and moved over to the desk, where he began putting the spool on the recorder. "I have all I want for the moment. I will make further demands later."

Clay also rose and went over to the girl. "I see no reason," he said, "why you cannot have your own suite for the time being. As long as you do not leave the city—which you hardly will with so many Martians on guard—you can have temporary liberty."

Thalia gave an uncomprehending look and said nothing.

Clay reached down and took her arm.

"Come with me," he requested. "I will see you past the guards."

She got to her feet and he opened the door for her. Lexas looked after them with a frown, but he could do nothing to stop them leaving together. The guards in the corridor would nail him immediately.

So, in silence, Clay kept his hand on the girl as they went along the wide passage outside — then presently he turned into an ante-room and shut the door.

"Clay, what does all this mean?" she burst out immediately. "I gave away all the secrets because you told me to trust you, but I cannot see . . . . ."

"You did exactly the right thing, dearest." Clay's smile, in the face of Lexas, looked hideous—but his arm about her shoulders was gentle enough. "Lexas is quite convinced you gave everything away because of torture: I know you did it because I asked you to . . . ."

"But for why? I don't see . . . ."

"You will in time. It's too involved to explain now. You once said I had courage: now I am convinced that you have it too, and implicit faith in me. I shan't let you down, Thalia, though I've a long way to go yet . . . .Of one thing you can be assured. I have the mastery of myself. My brain is purely that of Clay Drew, with no more disturbing influences from the alien bloodstream. Which means I can think clearly what I'm doing, and which also means you are more to me than anything else in the Universe."

"Do you suppose Lexas will revert to type and hate me, as he did when he was himself? I hope desperately that he will, because nothing terrifies me more than the thought of mariage to him. He has threatened that much, as you know."

Clay reflected, then he said, "The marriage may take place, if it is necessary to develop my plans, but you have my word on it, Thalia, that come what may he will never possess you."

There was bafflement in Thalia's green eyes.

"Clay, can you not tell me something of what you plan to do ? It is so hard just to be blindly obedient."

"I know, but it's necessary. Amongst those machines whose secrets you have revealed there is one which can read the brain. Lexas might take it into his head to read yours somehow, and if he did and saw exactly what I am aiming to do, what then ?. No, dearest, it is better that I do not tell you anything. Just go on trusting me until I can bring this nightmare to an end."

"You could do it now," Thalia said, with a sigh. "You are the ruler—so-called. One word from you and Lexas could be killed".

"Which would mean what ?" Clay asked. "I would never be able to reveal my real identity to the remaining Martians because, once I did so, they would destroy me. Further, I could never marry you or have progeny because this body is not that of an Earthman. As I am now we can never mate. That is the only reason why I have allowed Lexas such freedom up to now. I will break him, though, when I have my plan complete . . . ."

For a moment there was silence, Thalia's eyelids drooping sleepily.

"You have gone through quite enough," Clay decided, leading her towards the door. "Come with me and I'll see you safely as far as your suite. After that remain there until you hear something further from me."

When he returned to his headquarters office Clay found the Martian sitting before the silent recorder, busy making notes. He glanced up at Clay's entry.

"About time you returned," Lexas snapped. "How do you suppose I can leave here without you being present ? I'd be shot on the spot."

"I shall go and come as I choose," Clay responded. "Since I have your body I may as well have your privileges as well".

Lexas compressed his lips for a moment and then shrugged.

"Well, probably you are right," he admitted. "We are both in each others hands. What I require now is safe conduct to a suite of rooms until—as far as the people are aware —you have 'decided what to do with me.' Actually you will await my further instructions."

"I gather," Clay said slowly, looking at the notebook Lexas closed, "that you have been studying the secrets her Highness imparted ?"

"Naturally. I have taken down all the main details so I can ponder them. At a later date much of the information will be put to good use. My immediate concern is the construction of 'flying saucer' space machines—of which I now have all the details, and synthesis. The latter secret I learned some time ago, as you are aware. The recording itself I can now destroy."

"I think not," Clay said deliberately, taking one of the guns from his belt and pointing it. "Get yours hands off that recorder, Lexas."

"You can't shoot me without spoiling things for yourself," Lexas said briefly.

"I'm quite willing to do that to stop you getting everything your own way. You can save me the necessity, and yourself some pain, by getting out of here—and quickly ! In fact I'll see that you do !"

Clay switched on the desk intercom and spoke into it briefly in Martian. Presently a guard came in and Clay turned to him.

"Take the Earthman back to the prison and keep him there," he ordered.

Lexas stared blankly, then fury contorted his features.

"If you think you can order me around you're mad !" he shouted, whipping up his notebook. "I won't stand for . . . ."

"You'll do as you're told," Clay interrupted. "You can take your notebook. I'm not interested in it."

Though he was plainly puzzled Lexas took the book nevertheless, then with a glare he left the room with the

guard behind him. Clay considered for a moment then from
the main laboratory he summoned the chief technician. The
man came after an interval, a tall, middle-aged Atlantean
with an uncompromising stare in his blue eyes.

"I have something special I wish you to arrange," Clay
said. "I have decided to contact Earth by short-wave. Get
everything arranged so that I can make a transmission, and
receive an answer."

"I am sorry, Lexas, but I refuse to do it," the man
answered, his jaw setting stubbornly. "In fact I will not
do anything which helps you to jeopardise us and further your
own ambitions."

"So that's it ?" Clay gave a grim smile. Then he
leaned intently across the desk. "I observe you are very
loyal to your race, my friend, and to your princess."

"With reason. I am the chief scientist and I have a res-
ponsibilty. I would rather die than do anything which might
help you . . . . Only I shall not die because I know too much
which is of use."

Clay pondered for a moment, then making up his mind
he wrote a note swiftly and put it in a sealed envelope. He
handed it over.

"The Princess Thalia is in her suite,". he said. "Take
this to her and wait for an answer, then come back to me."

"Since when have I become a messenger ?" the scientist
demanded.

"On this occasion I think you will find it worthwhile."

The scientist did not look at all convinced, but he took
the note just the same and departed. Clay waited through
a long interval ; then the scientist returned. His entire manner was different. There was profound deference in his
attitude.

"Excellency, I did not know !" he exclaimed. "That is,
not until the Princess Thalia told me you are the Earthman.
From you appearance and manner I assumed . . . ."

"I said what I did to make sure of your loyalty," Clay
explained. "You, like the rest of the Atlanteans, may as

well know the truth, then you can work with me. In any case the surgeons know the facts. Lexas himself will not reveal the truth to his own people for fear of being disbelieved —as he would be—and killed. That is why I sent the note to her Highness, asking her to verify who I really am. Now do I get that short wave radio ?"

"You did not mention it to her Highness ?"

"No, Excellency. Should I have done ?"

"I would prefer not," Clay said. "She is not altogether in agreement with what I propose doing, but I am convinced it is for the best. How long will it take you to fix things for me ?"

"I can make the necessary preparations within half an hour."

"I will be with you then," Clay promised. "I have other matters to attend to in the interval."

The scientist nodded and left the room. Clay sat considering the recorder for a moment or two, then he switched it on and listened to the playback in Thalia's tired reluctant voice. He had just come to the end when a laboratory assistant arrived.

"I am asked to inform you, Excellency, that everything is ready," he announced.

Clay got to his feet. "Good. And remember, my friend, I am not to be addressed as 'Excellency.' I am Lexas, and don't forget it. Bring that recorder with you, please."

Clay led the way out of the headquarters and to the exterior where a conveyance, presumably the one the technician had used, was standing. In fifteen minutes Clay was in the laboratory, but because of the presence of the Martian guards the Atlanteans merely glanced at him and turned away in apparent disdain.

"You men . . . ." And Clay looked at the guards. "Take up duty in the corridor. I have a private matter to discuss with these Technicians."

His order was obeyed promptly ; then when the last of the guards had gone the head technician came over quickly.

"This way, Excellency," he directed, and Clay nodded
and motioned the junior scientist who was carrying the
recorder. His superior looked at it in some curiosity.

"I am broadcasting this entire recording to Earth," Clay
explained, settling in the chair before the complicated radio
apparatus. "First I have to contact the right quarter—and
get myself believed. After that . . . Anyway, first get me
through to Earth."

The scientist did not waste time asking the why and
wherefore. Satisfied that Clay was acting in the interests
of the race as a whole he switched on the equipment, studied
the meters, then presently nodded and indicated the microphone a foot from Clay's mouth.

"Calling Earth," Clay intoned, in deliberate English.
"This is Mars calling Earth. Come in any station which can
hear me. Over to you . . . ."

The loudspeaker overhead hummed with clear, undis-
torted power but no response came forth, even after allowing
several minutes for the speed-of-light transmission back and
forth over the 40-million mile gulf.

"You are sure everything is in order ?" Clay quesitoned.

"Definitely so, Excellency," the head scientist assured
him. "This short wave transmission will easily reach Earth
in clear volume, penetrating the Heaviside Layer as all short
waves do. Listen to this from Earth—normal broadcasting."

Switches clicked and another loudspeaker came into life,
and with it a variety of sounds. Gradually they were sliced
up by controls into music, voices in various languages, the
Morse of ships at sea, the weather forecasts of Met. offices. It
gave Clay a queer nostalgic feeling to listen to them.

"I'll try again," he said, motioning for silence—and once
more he intoned deliberately. And not only once more, but
several times . . . . then suddenly there came an answer, as
clear as though it were only in the next building. For a
moment Clay was astonished at the radio wizardy of the
scientists grouped around him.

"Message received, Mars. Go ahead. Meters prove

your communication is not a hoax. We have a reading of over thirty eight million miles. Explain please. Over."

"This is Clayton Drew, of London, speaking from Mars," Clay explained deliberately. "My disappearance will probably be known to the London police. If not my firm of engineers—Harton and Linfield of North London—should be contacted . . . ." And he went into the full details of his capture from Helvellyn by Kladnor within the flying saucer.

"At the moment I am fighting a difficult battle alone," he concluded. "The details are too numerous to hand on to you. My reason for contacting Earth is to give warning . . . . To which radio station am I speaking ? You use English. Over."

"Mount Wilson Long Range Experimental Station in California," came the response. "What is the warning you wish to give, Mr. Drew ? Over."

"Before very long—maybe a matter of weeks, or months at the most—Earth will be invaded, Clay responded. "Heading the invasion will be a Martian looking exactly like an Earthman—and indeed exactly like me. In fact every Martian in the armada will look identical. The women for their part will be patterened after the face and figure of one Princess Thalia who is under the domination of the Martians . . . . All this is too complex for your immediate attention. What I wish you to do is prepare for the trouble that is coming. I have here a recording in detail of various scientific weapons, which if they can be constructed in time, en masse, will destroy these invaders in their 'flying saucers' before they can get a foothold. Can you arrange for a world-wide hook-up to important scientists so they can record and take notes of the information I wish to transmit. Over."

"I don't doubt that it can be arranged, Mr. Drew, but it is not within my province to say so. I will make all the necessary contacts immediately. How am I to call you back ? Over."

Clay glanced questioningly at the head scientist and he said quickly.

"We will leave our equipment open for reception constantly. All he will need to do is speak : we shall hear him."

Clay gave a nod and relayed the information to Earth,
then he switched off and rubbed his great hands in satisfaction.

"Which settles that," he said. "Keep this recording here
safely, and I will see to it that none of the guards are allowed
in here. They would think a good deal if they suddenly
heard an Earth transmission coming through."

"The moment anything happens, Excellency, we will
advise you," the scientist promised.

"Good enough." Clay got to his feet. "You'll find me
the headquarters. I'm going to rest for awhile."

CHAPTER SEVEN.

SYNTHETIC PRINCESS.

Apparently things moved fast on Earth, for in another three hours, as he was aroused from a deep and refreshing sleep, Clay learned that contact had been made. He went immediately to the laboratory and played back the recording —three times, until he was satisfied that on Earth it had been re-recorded satisfactorily. Then a new voice came through which identified itself as the President of the British Association of Science and Interplanetary Research.

"We cannot be too grateful to you, Mr. Drew, for the risk you have taken to get warning through to us," he said, "and you can rest assured that these valuable instruments and mechanisms can be duplicated by our engineers and scientists. You have, in fact, handed on to us instruments far beyond anything we have yet devised, except theoretically."

"I know," Clay responded, a trifle anxiously. "And I wish it to be made absolutely clear, sir, that all this information is solely for the protection of Earth against invasion. I leave it to you, and others, to see that no information leaks out into the wrong hands."

"Every precaution will be taken, Mr. Drew. Thank you again, and good luck. You will be hearing how things progress."

Clay switched off and then got to his feet. He turned to the head scientist.

"Under no circumstances," Clay said, "is the Princess Thalia to know what I have done. She expressly forbade it."

"But why ?" the scientist asked blankly. "What better way could there be to send all these accursed Martians into a death trap ?"

"There is no better way, which is why I have done it. Her Highness would not reveal her secrets to me of her own free will, in the first instance — so the only way was by 'persuasion' which she believed I allowed, to fool Lexas. I got the information I needed. Thalia thinks Earthlings will fight each other with such information. I, having lived amongst them, do not think they will. Anyway, the decision is made now."

With that Clay took his departure, with the assurances of the scientist that he would communicate if anything developed. Clay returned to his headquarters, rested again for several hours, and then after a freshening up and a meal he went to the surgical laboratories. In some surprise the head surgeon came forward to greet him.

"You have come for a reaction test, Excellency ?" he asked, but Clay shook his head.

"I don't need one. I've settled down perfectly as far as my brain is concerned and Clay Drew is in absolute control of this clumsy carcase. No. I'm here for another reason —and a vital one. I wish you to attempt something really complicated in surgery. Complicated, but essential. The life of her Highness may hang on it."

"If you will outline your requirements, Excellency . . ."

"Just like that, eh ?" Clay gave a grim smile. "Well, here it is. I want a synthetic image of her Highness, down to the last detail. I want it without a single fault. Duplicated down to the fingerprints. I also want, instead of a brain, a mechanical radio mechanism which will respond over a thirty mile radius to orders given mentally."

The surgeon did not appear very much taken aback. Instead he pondered for a while.

"To create an image of her Highness is not difficult, of

course," he responded.   "Provided, that is, that she can be brought here."

"I can arrange that.   Tell me, is the job painless for her ?"

"Perfectly.   She will have no more discomfort than if she were being photographed."

"Then it can be done ?"

"As far as the surgical part is concerned, yes, but the matter of the radio brain is something only the scientific laboratory can manage.   I would suggest, Excellency, that you discover from the head scientist what can be done."

So Clay did and was assured that a system could be worked out, a radio-receptor to take the place of a brain and to be sensitive to telepathic waves, which waves would cause reactions when received.   After that, as in the case of a remote controlled 'plane or vehicle, different connections would go into action and move corresponding muscles or limbs.   In truth, the duplicated Thalia would be a perfect model, but obeying only the orders of "her" controller.

This part of the business settled, Clay's next move was to visit Thalia herself.   He found her in her suite, just finishing a meal.   She looked at him expectantly as he was admitted by the Martian guard.

"You're coming with me, Thalia," he told her as she rose.   "My plan is working out nicely so far, but it has got to the stage where you come into it.   I want you to come to the surgical laboratory and have yourself duplicated."

She withdrew quickly.   "You don't mean that horrible vivisection plan which Lexas had in mind ? No, Clay, I . . . ."

"Nothing like that, dearest," he murmured.   "Great cosmos, do you think I'd subject you to that ?   There's nothing painful about it, and once it's over you will be removed from all possible danger at the hands of Lexas, and your image will take over for you."

"You really mean that ?"   There was eager expectancy in Thalia's green eyes.

"Sure as I'm here.   What I aim to do is control this

potential image of you so that Lexas thinks it's the real thing.
He may even marry it. Anyway, that has to be worked out
later. The point now is that you must come to the surgery."

Thalia nodded. "I'll come right away. Just give me
time to change."

She hurried from the room and Clay waited patiently.
When at length she returned she was wearing a serviceable
garment of slacks and blouse in one piece, a broad sash
about her waist. Clay opened the door and escorted her down
the corridor to the exterior, returning the salutes of the Martians as he went.

Before long they had reached the surgery and the head
surgeon bowed deferentially.

"Everything is ready," he said. "All you have to do,
Highness, is sit in the chair there . . . ." And he indicated
one which had queerly fashioned electrodes fixed to it. It
reminded Clay most unpleasantly of an electric chair.

"There is nothing to fear," the surgeon smiled, and
motioned.

Thalia, after a moment's hesitancy, walked forward and
then settled herself. She said nothing as wires were affixed
to her limbs by suction cups. At the end of five minutes it
was difficult to see her, so numerous were the terminals. Clay
came over to her and watched the proceedings.

"Now," the surgeon said, when his colleague had
wheeled a massive projector into position, "I will briefly explain what will happen. These terminals, Highness, will
record all external impressions, and the projector here will
receive X-ray impressions of your internal structure. Instead
of the result being photographic it will be vibrational. Any
body which lives has vibratory frequency. These frequencies
will be passed on to that mass of synthetic plasma there."

The surgeon nodded to a shapeless flesh-coloured mound
of dough-like substance in a spotless porcelain bath nearby.
To the bath the electrode wires were connected.

"Just as a negative develops under the action of chemicals, so this plasma will pattern itself under the vibrations it

receives," the surgeon explained. "The only part which will not be duplicated is the brain. A space will be left in the skull. What is the position in regard to that, Excellency?" he asked, looking at Clay.

"It's all fixed," Clay responded. "You do your part and the scientific laboratory will do the rest."

The surgeon nodded and closed a master switch. Power began to throb nearby. A dim, hardly visible beam came from the projector and enveloped the seated girl from head to toe. She herself was not in the least uncomfortable. In fact she—and Clay—began to wonder if things were working out correctly, until they saw the plasma in the bath was changing. In silent fascination they watched it.

From being utterly without form it began to extend and shape itself, like clay in the hands of an invisible sculptor.

Gradually, recognisable limbs took shape; the blank emptiness of face flowed and drifted into features. Hair began to appear on the head. Eyebrows slowly merged out of nowhere. It was to Clay the most startling feat of surgery he had ever witnessed. Thalia, to whom synthetic patterning was nothing new, remained motionless as she watched herself being copied in every detail. Whatever embarrassment she might have felt at the final nude image which remained, was prevented by the clouds of vaporising steam which began to fill the bath when the instruments were switched off.

"There it is," the chief surgeon said. "You, Highness, exact to the last whorl and loop on your fingerends, exact to the number of hairs on your head."

"Is it alive?" Clay asked, peering though the haze.

"Without a brain, no. Had it been given a brain it would be alive as you or I, but it would only respond to spoken orders, not mental ones—and only then after long training. The radio-brain you have in mind should complete the matter. All that remains is for this image to be transported to the scientific laboratory."

Clay thought for a moment as the surgeon removed the terminals from the girl and she stood up from the chair.

"It will have to be conveyed in a case," Clay said. "Nobody save the scientists must know of this : it would endanger my plan."

This was a matter which was soon solved. A long, coffin-like affair was brought forth and the two surgeons raised the limp figure from the bath and laid it within the case. Then the lid was clamped into position, locked, and the combination key handed to Clay.

"Her Highness and I will go on ahead," he said. "Have the case sent over."

Returning to his attitude of being the captor Clay marched down the corridor outside, holding Thalia's arm as she walked beside him. They had been in the scientific laboratory just long enough to explain how successful the surgical operation had been when the case arrived, carried by two Atlantean attendants. The lid opened, the head scientist looked down on the silent, dead body thoughtfully.

"A magnificent job," he said at length, with complete detachment. "Her Highness in detail."

Clay nodded. Thalia herself was looking on from a distance, a flush in her cheeks as she realised the image was a mirror of herself. For her to feel actually uncomfortable was impossible, however. The head scientist was too analytical to be swayed by emotion.

"I have the radio brain ready," he said. "It is simply a matter of opening the image's skull, placing the equipment inside it, and then linking it up. Afterwards I will show you the apparatus by which mental control can be achieved."

Clay did not say anything. He went across to Thalia, drew forth a chair for her, then stood close by and watched as the master scientists went into action.

One hour—two hours—passed, and in that time the radio brain had been placed in position and its various terminals connected to the artificial nerve system of the "creature," the main wires being along the synthetic backbone. This task finished the skull was resealed, hair regrafted across the joint, and then clothes were added. Created synthetically from chemicals they were draped on the image, duplicating exactly the outfit Thalia herself was wearing. When it was all over she watched in wonder as the woman, left to stand on "her" own two feet, slowly opened her eyes.

Clay looked away from her and saw that the head scientist was busy at his switchboard. He was completely silent, concentrating, and under the influence of his thoughts the image moved forward, bowed low before Thalia, and then studied her with clear green eyes.

"I am yours to obey, Highness," she said, in a voice which it was impossible to tell was not Thalia's own.

"It's a masterpiece !" Clay exulted. "I never saw such scientific wizardry in my life before."

"I am glad you are satisfied, Excellency," the surgeon replied. "If you will come to this switchboard I will show you how to control the creature."

Clay moved over quickly to the scientist's side, and Thalia stood beside him. They both surveyed the complicated apparatus with the viewing screen on the top.

"This has been exclusively made for this image," the scientist explained. "This magnetic plate absorbs whatever thoughts you give forth and transmits them to the radio brain of the image. The brain in turn actuates the muscles and various organs. On the screen on top of the board here you see exactly what 'she' sees, and this loudspeaker will give forth whatever her ears pick up. Thus you can control her at a distance by knowing exactly what 'she' is doing and what is being said to her."

"Couldn't be better," Clay said. "And this instrument has a thirty mile radius ?"

"Fifty if necessary."

"All I need," Clay decided. "Now I'll try and send 'her' back to Thalia's suite."

He sat and concentrated, the scientist and Thalia watching the screen along with him. The synthetic woman left the laboratory, then stopped as the Martain guards loomed up before her.

"I'd forgotten that," Clay said hastily, looking at the Martian's grim face in the screen and hearing his sharp questions.

He raced to the door, opened it, and looked at the guards down the corridor.

"Two of you men escort her Highness back to her suite," he ordered, and as they took hold of her he returned to the laboratory, settling again before the equipment. Under his orders the image began to walk, the guards holding 'her' arms. It was queer to see everything her eyes could see being reflected in the screen, to hear in the speaker the noises her ears were receiving.

Only when she had been left in her suite did Clay switch off and glance up in triumph.

"I fancy that our friend Lexas is in for a surprise if he plans to marry that!" he commented.

"There is one thing, though, which troubles me," Thalia said, thinking. "He plans to make a number of images, with me as the basic pattern, just as he plans to make a number of images from his—or rather your body, Clay, as the master-copy. What happens when the image of me is duplicated? The radio-brain may be revealed."

Clay gave a start. "Great heavens, I never thought of that possibility."

"Only one solution," Thalia said. "If there is the danger of the radio brain being duplicated in the copies, I shall have to be the model myself on that occasion, and find a way afterwards to escape, so that my image can take over again. There's nothing else for it."

"Surely it would be simpler to destroy Lexas and have done with it?" the head surgeon asked, puzzled. "I cannot see the reason for all this connivance . . . ."

"There are a lot of strings attached to it, my friend, too detailed to explain now," Clay interrupted. "The fact remains that he must be led to think his plans are successful. Only if he thinks that will he take the greater part of his race away from this planet . . . .Very well, Thalia," he

added, "you will have to do as you suggest, much though
I dislike it.   Until then we have to find somewhere where you
can be safely out of Lexas' reach."

"I would suggest the old underground burial mausoleums
deep under this city," the scientist said.

"The very place !" Thalia cried. "Nobody can ever find
me down there. I'll take concentrates and all the necessities
for living, and there I will stop until everything is worked
out, Clay—or at least until I'm needed."

"Can you be observed going there ?" Clay asked worriedly.

"Yes—but the answer is there."

Thalia nodded to the coffin-crate in which her image had
been brought.

"Excellent," the scientist murmured. "Bore invisible
air-holes in that, put her Highness in it together with provisions, and she can be transported in safety. The Martians
will merely think a dignitary has passed on and is being laid
to rest. They—the Martians guarding this building, I mean
—have already seen 'Thalia' leave, or at least they believe
they have.

So it was decided and the necessary provisions and other
requirements were quickly loaded into the "coffin." Then
Thalia herself lay down in it and smiled at Clay as he gazed
down on her.

"We're having a tough fight to throw out the enemy,
dearest," he murmured. "But we'll do it yet."

With that the air-holed lid was lowered down, and Clay
locked it, putting the key in his pocket. Afterwards, four
Atlantean laboratory attendants shouldered the case and, with
Clay at the head, left the laboratory and marched down the
corridor.   There were surprised glances from the Martian
guards, but no questions. With their ruler in charge nothing
could be said.

In fact everything fitted in. The guards had seen the
case brought in the first place, and now assumed that it had
then been empty. Now it probably contained a body, and

since it would belong to an Atlantean—judging by the size of the case—"Lexas" could not be expected to permit a funeral ceremony. He would not do anything more than see the coffin carried to the mausoleums.

Which was exactly what happened, the vast underground burial space being gained by a stairway which led downwards from the floor of the Temple in the city centre, where the more devout of the Atlanteans worshipped their own strange gods.

Down in the depths, in the unutterable silence of departed dignitaries in the bowels of Mars, the lid was unlocked and Thalia climbed out with Clay's assistance. She looked about her on the vasty spaces, but dimly lighted by the single atomic-torch Clay had brought for her.

"I hate leaving you here," he said. "It's—sepulchral."

"I'm not afraid," she answered simply. "The spirits of my ancestors will keep me company until you need me. The torch will last for a century if need be and I have all the food and drink I can need. Don't fear for me, Clay. Just carry on your battle. I'll be thinking of you."

He tugged a gun out of his belt and gave it to her.

"Just in case," he said. "And if only I hadn't this filthy body I'd give you a kiss for luck."

"Later perhaps," she said—so on that Clay had to leave it. His last vision of her as he headed for the stairway with the Atlanteans was of her waving slowly to him amidst the all-embracing shadows.

His own plans made, Clay had nothing further to do but wait for Lexas to decide upon some move. To this end he gave the guard in charge of Lexas instructions to bring immediately any request Lexas might make, and after two more Martian "days" had elapsed a message arrived. Lexas requried release to discuss matters with his "captor." And Clay promptly granted it.

The Martian only maintained his passive attitude until the headquarters door was closed and he and Clay were alone, then all his old arrogance returned.

"Thanks for the privilege of seeing you," he said dryly.
"I have spent the last few days studying the notes I made of
Thalia's recording. Now I am satisfied that I have a working knowledge of the various machines I am ready to go
into action. You will issue an order for two hundred 'saucer'
fliers to be built. They should be enough to hold all those
of my race I wish to take."

"Then ?" Clay asked, no emotion in his voice. .

"Then I shall require three hundred males of my race to
assemble in the surgical laboratory. Not all at once, but in
dozens at a time. As the chief surgeon creates synthetic
bodies, taking this body of mine—or rather yours—as the
master pattern, the brains of my colleagues will be transferred
to the synthetic men."

A thought stirred across Clay's mind, something he had
not so far considered.

"I assume, then, that the synthetic men will be made
with empty skulls, ready to receive the brains of the living
men upon completion ?"

"Naturally. I—or rather you—will instruct the head
surgeon to delete the brain duplication from the images."

"And the same will apply to Thalia ?" Clay asked
deliberately.

"Afterwards, yes. I require the men first."

There was a long pause as Clay pondered the matter.
This made things easier for him. The duplicate Thalia could
be used in the surgery after all. The radio mechanism which
formed her brain would not, in any event, be copied.

"Well ?" Lexas demanded. "Are you trying to be
stubborn, Earthman ?"

"No. I will do as you have asked."

"Which is something I do not quite understand," Lexas
said slowly musing. "If you refuse to give the orders I
have outlined there is nothing I can do of myself. You can
keep me imprisoned for as long as you wish, and all my
declarations that I am Lexas would avail me nothing. For
some time now I have been baffled by your behaviour. I

lost my master-card when you separated me from her Highness. As long as I had a hold over her you were willing to
obey me to save her from hurt. Now I am alone—and you
could have me destroyed. Or you could even have me taken
to the surgical laboratory and take your body back on the
pretext that you need it for the Earth invasion. You do none
of these things."

Clay gave a hard smile. "As I told you earlier, Lexas,
it no longer concerns me what you do to the Princess. She
no longer has any attraction for me. You can duplicate her,
take her to Earth, do what you like with her. I no longer
care. I am only following out your orders because I wish a
favour in return."

"What is it ?" Lexas asked briefly.

"I wish to go on living—here, in this body of yours. I
have grown accustomed to it. Because it is Martian there is
much about this planet which appeals to me . . . ." Clay
paused then added slowly, "In a word, Lexas, you and I by
our exchange of bodies have become closely inter-related.
We each possess something of the other. Instead of being
enemies why can't we co-operate ? I can show you many
things about Earth you do not understand : you, in return,
can reveal many things about Mars. I am prepared to stay
here whilst you invade Earth, and will keep the remaining
Martians in check. The Atlanteans which are left I will bring
to heel."

"And that is your main reason for co-operation ?" Lexas
asked, musing. "You suggest we be partners ?"

"I can think of no reason why we shouldn't."

"I find it hard to believe. In particular do I find it hard
to believe you no longer have any sentiment towards her
Highness."

"To prove it I will allow you to be with her whenever
you wish, starting the moment you leave this office. There
cannot be stronger proof than that."

"And marriage ?"

"I shall not stand in the way of it if you wish it."

Lexas was silent. It was perfectly obvious he was trying to discover underlying motives. Clay reached out to the switch-panel on his desk and depressed a button.

"Radio Control ?" he asked in Martian. "I am giving a short broadcast to the city. Inform me when the necessary hook-up has been made."

An assent floated through the loud-speaker. Clay looked at Lexas across the desk, but still the Martian had no comment to make. Then after a while Radio Control gave the all clear signal.

"My friends," Clay said, again in Martian, drawing the small microphone to him. "The time has come for an immense project to be undertaken. I have decided that we, of this world, shall invade Earth in the shortest possible time. All engineers of the Atlantean race will report to me for orders concerned with the building of space fliers. Everything will be sacrificed to that end. Also three hundred males and three hundred females of our own race will be required to form the space-machine crews. Upon them will rely the glory of conquering the third world. They will be selected in due course. I myself, your ruler, will not go to Earth."

Lexas looked up sharply, an ugly look crossing his face.

"Instead," Clay continued, "I am sending Clay Drew, the Earthman, whom I hold captive, and Her Highness the Princess Thalia, who is also being detained during my pleasure. They will be allowed to wed before they leave this planet . . . . I have had the opportunity of studying many secrets which the Princess has handed on to me, and one of those secrets is a machine for producing mental compulsion. So, into the brains of Clay Drew and her Highness will be impressed the orders I shall give—and you others will follow those orders to the letter. I shall stay here because I have much to do, and many Atlanteans have still to be subdued. One final word: Clay Drew is to be allowed absolute freedom wherever he is seen. I have granted him special permission."

With that Clay sat back in his chair and looked at Lexas

across the desk.

"That satisfy you that I mean it ?" he asked. "I've given you freedom to do as you wish, invented a seemingly logical reason for you and Thalia going to Earth, and also given myself the chance to remain here, as you. It would seem to me, Lexas, that our partnership is in being."

"Yes, it would seem so," the Martian agreed, though he still looked vaguely puzzled ; then apparently thrusting the problem to the back of his mind he took several sketches from his tunic, and then a wad of technical notes.

"This information is for the engineers," he explained. "I have worked it out from Thalia's notes. As regards the various machines in this underworld, they can be dismantled and I shall take them with me. It will be simpler to do that than try to reconstruct them on Earth, where there may not be the necessary materials."

"Which means you do not trust them to me ?"

"You can reconstruct. You have all the information you need from the recording Thalia 'made. I have not forgotten that."

"As you will," Clay shrugged. "From here on you had better leave all orders to me. You may do exactly as you wish, and that includes permission to be with her Highness without restriction. You will find her in her suite."

Lexas rose to his feet and then gave a slow nod.

"I wish," he said, pondering, "I could fathom what is at the back of that transplanted brain of yours, Earthman . . . ."

He said no more. Leaving the office he closed the door. Clay waited for a moment, then he pressed the switch which automatically kept the door locked. Raising the intercom-phone he contacted the scientific laboratory. The voice of the Head Scientist responded.

"Get to work immediately on the image," Clay instructed. "You heard my broadcast ?"

"I did, yes." The scientist waited respectfully.

"Lexas is on his way now to see Thalia. Make her reactions stubborn. She must revile and loathe Lexas in every possible way if she is to seem convincing . . . . There are no guards in the laboratory, are there ?"

"No, Excellency. They are obeying your order to guard the outside of the laboratory only."

"Good enough. Keep somebody controlling Thalia non-stop from here on. I'll see you personally later. I have much to attend to.."

He switched off, to be almost immediately informed that the Atlantean engineers had arrived for their orders. He moved the switch which released the door lock and sat watching the grim-faced men as they came across the big chamber.

Chapter Eight.

INVASION ARMADA.

For Clay, the days which followed were as hectic as they
had formerly been quiet. His plotting and planning, involved as it had been, was now commencing to work itself
out—and as far as he knew, Lexas had not come upon anything to set his suspicions working in a definite direction.

Night and day control of Thalia from the laboratory
made of her a living, breathing creature who resisted every
one of Lexas' advances, until—by order from Clay—she
began to weaken her resistance a little, a necessity if the
"marriage" was to take place.

Clay visited the real Thalia whenever he had the chance
and explained details to date ; then, assured she was still safe
and comfortable, he went back to his post.

The Atlantean engineering shops were working overtime,
on the construction of "flying saucer" space machinces—
which were equipped with every needful thing, including the
deadliest of weapons, and were then transported to the surface of the planet. Whilst this was going on the selected men
and women of the Martian race were directed to the surgical
laboratory and the brain transference took place into the synthetic bodies which had already been created. Thanks to
the connivance of the surgeon, and the fact that no brains
were needed in the images of Thalia, the radio-brain her
duplicate possessed was not even suspected by Lexas, despite
the fact that—using his new found freedom—he was present

at the "copying."

So, by degrees, the giant machines of the Atlanteans were dismantled and stowed away aboard the waiting fliers. The apparatus which controlled Thalia's double was moved secretly to the mausoleum where the girl herself was still hiding and two technicians were put in charge of it, to work in relays. For power, an underground feed line was tapped.

Clay, too, was at work on his own. He made all the necessary arrangements for the "marriage" of Lexas to Thalia's double, and had it performed publically so that Atlanteans and Martians alike could see it. This done he considered his plan about finished. It was generally supposed that the wedded couple were under hypnotic control and that they would lead the invading army to victory.

So, to Clay's relief, there at last came the time for the invaders' departure. He, with members of the Martian race who had been left behind, went up to the surface of the planet to watch the procession of "saucers" climbing from the yellow ochre of the desert into the void. Once it was over he returned below, parted company with the Martians, and went straight to the surgical laboratory.

"Everything ready for me ?" he asked the head surgeon.

"Yes, Excellency. As you requested I made one extra image of Clay Drew and kept it in suspended animation for you. It will be a simple job to put your brain into it."

"Then I can be myself again," Clay said, grinning with his hideous Martian mouth. "It's a surprise for her Highness, otherwise I'd have gone to her straight away . . . All the important Martians have departed, my friend. If some of those who remain see me I shall explain myself for the moment as being one of them who was left behind. They will believe it. In any event the situation is well in hand. There are more Atlanteans down here than there are Martians. Some equipment has been saved with which we can subdue them."

The surgeon nodded and then motioned impartially to

the operating table. Clay laid himself upon it, still smiling
in satisfaction, then he relaxed into unconsciouness as the
anaesthetic claimed him . . . .He woke again to a feeling of
lightness, but to the blessed realisation that he had his own
physique, or at least an exact duplicate of it, once again.

The powerful restoratives did their work rapidly. He sat
up as the straps were released and the surgeon and his assistant considered him smilingly.

"It would seem that your battle is nearly over, Excellency," the chief surgeon comemented. "The invaders will
be dealt with as they aproach Earth, and you have the Princess safely here, and waiting . . . . What are your directions
concerning Lexas' carcase ?"

"Keep it in pickle," Clay said, after thinking it over
"I don't suppose it will ever be needed again, but precaution
doesn't cost anything."

He waited a moment or two until the last fog of his
recovery had passed off, then dressed in clothes identical to
the images which were now somewhere in space, and armed
with a single gun, he left the surgery and made his way to
the street outside. To his satisfaction there were no Martians
in sight. Their immensely depleted numbers--in the underworld at least—made the city seem empty.

Clay took no chances just the same, even though he was
sure he could lie his way out of a spot if he got into one.
As things worked out he succeeded, by using every short cut,
in reaching the Atlantean temple safely, wherein lay the entrance to the mausoleum.

Once he had gained the steps which led below he raced
down them in the darkness, knowing his way by heart.
moving with the speed which the slight gravity gave his new
found body. As he sped along the tunnel which entered on
to the mausoleum where lay Thalia's retreat he looked
anxiously for the light of her atomic torch.

There was none.

Puzzled, he kept on hurrying. He knew the light ought
to be there, chiefly for the technicians to see the instrument

which controlled Thalia's double, unless by now she was beyond the fifty-mile limit and the instrument was no longer of use. In which case the technicians might be sleeping . . . .

These thoughts chased one another through Clay's brain as he gained the steps leading to the big vault where Thalia ought to be—but he met nothing but the darkness.

"Thalia !" he shouted hoarsely, feeling his way down the steps. "Thalia, are you there ?"

The echoes of his own voice came back. Not even any answer from the technicians. He hurried across the dark space to where he had last left the girl—and collided with the heavy case which had been used to transport her hither. He felt around him, and came upon something else which yielded in his grip. It was cold flesh. A moment's investigation with his hands satisfied him it was the dead body of one of the technicians. Moving around, he came presently to the second man, also dead—but of the girl there was no trace.

Working without light was his greatest difficulty so, consumed with dire forebodings, he raced back to the temple again, took away one of the eternally burning candles, and then came back into the mausoleum, keeping his hand round the flame to prevent draught from extinguishing it.

The yellow glimmer told him a grim story. The bodies of the two technicians had been blasted through with ray pistol charges. The instrument for controlling Thalia's double was smashed to pieces. There was every sign of a savage struggle. And of Thalia there was no trace.

Clay stood looking about him, his heart beating fast— then he suddenly caught sight of a sheet of metal-foiling, the Martian equivalent of notepaper, impaled on one of the broken bars of the smashed telepathic wave instrument.

Clay snatched it, unfolded it, and read, ·
"Earthman,

"You are not as clever as you imagine, though I compliment you on the trick you tried to pull with the duplicate of her Highness. You overlooked one thing, however. When the telepathic-wave equipment was moved to the mausoleum, taking its power from an underground feed-line, it had to rely on just that one source of power, instead of the atomic generators of the laboratory. It meant that when the city was working at full pressure on the construction of 'saucers' for the invasion, all power was drained to the uttermost. That caused your telepathic equipment to drop its output. There were long periods when the synthetic Thalia did not respond at all.

"Already suspicious of you—and having my freedom to roam—I investigated. I followed you to the mausoleum on one occasion : on another I satisfied myself that the real Thalia was hidden here. At the desired moment I abducted here and put her aboard my own particular space machine. Her double I shall dispose of in space. Those with me will be none the wiser. But I have Thalia, the greatest of all bargaining weapons, and I shall keep her !

"In any case, Earthman, the influence over the duplicate Thalia would have ceased when the limit of the telepathic-amplifier's power had been reached. Had that happened I should have returned to deal with you, braving what few scientific weapons you may have in the underworld. You fancied, I take it, that with my armada on its way I would not turn back even if I did discover Thalia was just a dummy. How greatly you underestimate me !

"As things are I shall continue on my way to Earth and conquer it, and I shall marry Thalia under the pretext of a second ceremony conforming to Earth standards.

"If you elect to stay behind on Mars and subdue my few remaining colleagues with the assistance of your Atlantean friends, all well and good. In any event I shall return later and crush you utterly. If you elect to follow me in the vain hope of achieving victory and reclaiming Thalia you will be destroyed. You are not a fool, Earthman. That is why I believe you will realise when you are beaten.

Lexas."

For several minutes Clay stood motionless, reading the message again and pondering its implications. It meant more than failure on his part: it meant utter tragedy. With Lexas was Thalia, and both of them were in ignorance of the fact that on Earth there was waiting for them the mightiest scientific defensive ever assembled on one planet. The armada would be destroyed, and with it Thalia too must perish.

"Yet if I radio to Earth and tell them some story to make them withdraw their defences I shall betray them—lay the whole planet open to destruction in the hope of saving Thalia. And even then I might not accomplish it. She once said she preferred death to marrying Lexas . . . . On the other hand, if I chase out into space and try and save her I shall be wiped out. What can one machine do against that armada ?"

Clay was silent for a long time after his soliloquy, then gradually he made up his mind.

"I have only one course. A second armada must be built with what machinery we have left. Weapons must be manufactured. Every Atlantean must come with me in an effort to find Thalia and save her. It may be useless, but there is also the chance that she might escape the defensive action. That is my only hope. I can radio Earth and tell them the vicious twist of circumstances. Something might be worked out . . . ."

Clay clenched his fists and looked about him. "I'm not beaten yet, Lexas," he said slowly. "Perhaps the battle is only just beginning . . . ."

And with new purpose in his movements he picked up the candle and began striding away towards the mausoleum staircase.